# THE DEVIL IN THE BUSH

# THE DEVIL
# IN THE BUSH

## Matthew Head

FELONY & MAYHEM PRESS • NEW YORK

*All the characters and events portrayed in this work are fictitious.*

THE DEVIL IN THE BUSH

A Felony & Mayhem mystery

PRINTING HISTORY
First edition (Simon & Schuster): 1945
First Felony & Mayhem edition: 2005
This Felony & Mayhem edition: 2017

Library of Congress Cataloging-in-Publication Data

Names: Head, Matthew, 1907-1985, author.
Title: The devil in the bush / Matthew Head.
Description: Felony & Mayhem edition. | New York : Felony & Mayhem
Press,
   2017. | "A Felony & Mayhem mystery."
Identifiers: LCCN 2016058783 | ISBN 9781631941085
Subjects: | GSAFD: Mystery fiction.
Classification: LCC PS3505.A53196 D48 2017 | DDC 813/.54--dc23
LC record available at https://lccn.loc.gov/2016058783

I feel that *The Devil in the Bush* demands a foreword on the principle that assault is the best defense. Readers who know the Belgian Congo will find inaccuracies in the story; what I want to say is that—so far as I know, of course—the inaccuracies are intentional, and unimportant. For instance, there was no point in referring to half a dozen native tongues when Lingala could be used as a blanket term to cover them all. Also, when phrases in Lingala occur I have invented words, imitating the sounds of that language as I heard it spoken without ever understanding it. My fictional M'buku rebellion was suggested by the actual Kwango rebellion, but is not intended to be a reproduction of it.

The characters and events in this story are as fictional as the characters and events in any story can be, with the exception of the houseboy I have called Albert. Albert is a composite of the Messrs. N'kodio Albert and M'fanza André, who delighted and cared for me during eight months in the Congo. I don't think they would mind my writing them up.

I am fond enough of this story to give it a dedication, and although it might appropriately be given to Jimmy and Julia, to Tom and Al, to the LaCostes or the Guy de Brabandères or to Frederick Hendrickx and the other people at Ineac-Mulungu, this book really belongs

TO KATHERINE.

M.H.
Southwest Pacific
February 5, 1945

Matthew Head is the pseudonym of John Edwin Canaday (1907-1985), an art critic and writer. Canaday was a *New York Times* art critic for seventeen years and authored several monographs of visual art scholarship. Late in life he wrote restaurant reviews for the *Times*. Under the "Matthew Head" pen name, he wrote seven mystery novels, three of which are set in the Congo and based on his experiences traveling there as a French translator in 1943. Canaday was born in Fort Scott, Kansas; his series sleuth, Dr. Mary Finney, is from Fort Scott as well.

The icon above says you're holding a copy of a book in the Felony & Mayhem "Vintage" category. These books were originally published prior to about 1965, and feature the kind of twisty, ingenious puzzles beloved by fans of Agatha Christie and John Dickson Carr. If you enjoy this book, you may well like other "Vintage" titles from Felony & Mayhem Press.

NGAIO MARSH (continued)
*Night at the Vulcan*
*Spinsters in Jeopardy*
*Scales of Justice*
*Death of a Fool*
*Singing in the Shrouds*
*False Scent*
*Hand in Glove*
*Dead Water*
*Killer Dolphin*
*A Clutch of Constables*
*When in Rome*
*Tied Up in Tinsel*
*Black as He's Painted*
*Last Ditch*
*A Grave Mistake*
*Photo Finish*
*Light Thickens*
*Collected Short Mysteries*

LENORE GLEN OFFORD
*Skeleton Key*
*The Glass Mask*
*The Smiling Tiger*
*My True Love Lies*

PHILIP YOUNGMAN CARTER
*Mr Campion's Farthing*
*Mr Campion's Falcon*

For more about these books, and other Felony & Mayhem titles, or to place an order, please visit our website at:

www.FelonyAndMayhem.com

# THE DEVIL IN THE BUSH

# CHAPTER ONE

## *Hangman*

THAT WAS A WONDERFUL JOB I had in 1943. That was a war year of course, and it was a war job, but this isn't a war story. It's the story of the murders at the Congo-Ruzi station. I was twenty-eight years old, and while I had done a lot of the usual summer travel that all University people do, I had never worked in a foreign country before, much less even been along the equator. My inspection of the Congo-Ruzi station was the littlest part of my job, but what happened to me personally because of going there was the biggest thing that happened to me during all the time I spent in the Congo. I can't give it a fancy telling but I can set down what happened.

I suppose the story really begins the first day of July in the commercial car on the way to Bafwali, because that was when I decided that when we got to Bafwali I would get out and see the town instead of taking the afternoon off to rest, the way the other passengers always did. There were nine of

1

us in the car, including the native driver. I was in a jump-seat, no leg room, but it was all right with me because I could look out and watch the jungle go by—the bush they call it, not the jungle, but it's jungle all the same. In that part of the country the natives still wear feathers and carry spears. Some of them were smeared with white paint and all of them were tattooed in patterns of welts all over their bodies. The old women trotted along the roads bent half double under loads of wood, their razor-strop breasts hanging and swaying. When they heard the car coming they would scramble into the ditch by the side of the road and press themselves into the thick green edge of the bush while we went past. There were young girls, too, with breasts like hard cones, with purplish nipples as big as eggs, and long shiny spindly legs ending in sharp buttocks that stuck straight out behind. Then all of a sudden we would come out of the green bush into hot dry savannah country, and there wouldn't be any more natives, but from time to time we would see a herd of ante-lopes bounding off through the high grass, and once, far off, there was a herd, or school, or tribe, or whatever you would call it, of baboons.

All of us in the car were hot and tired and sweaty and becoming unbearable to one another. We had been driving for three days, from Stanleyville. With my government priori-ties I could have gone by plane, and I had done it as far as Stanleyville, but I wanted to go the rest of the way by car to see more of the country. I was the only one in the car who gave a damn about it. The rest of the passengers were hard-ened Congolese and all they wanted was to forget they were in Africa. In the front seat beside the driver was a young Belgian mother with two little girls, about six and eight. The little girls would chatter along in Lingala until their mother noticed it, then she would give them a careless, habitual slap and they would go into French. But pretty soon they would lapse back into Lingala again and when their mother noticed it she would give them another slap. I was glad when we got to Bafwali.

The meal at the rest house was worse than anything Stanley or Livingstone had ever had to eat, and my bed was hard and the straw in the mattress smelled moldy. The mosquito net had big holes in it and I knew I was going to be eaten alive that night. I only lay down long enough to smoke one cigarette, then I got up and went out to see the town. Bafwali has the reputation for being a pleasant town, but it's all relative, and what they mean must be that it is possible to sustain life in Bafwali without being in actual pain twenty-four hours a day. The site was pretty enough, with low hills rolling away on every side, and here and there you could see houses where you could tell some kind of decent life was led. But the town was all sprawled out and I soon got tired of the occasional houses and the occasional native stores typical of hundreds of other native stores I had seen, smelling of cheap cotton prints and dried salt fish. When I saw the Airways house open, I went in to cool off and rest up.

There were planes the first and fifteenth of every month shuttling between the eastern and western borders of the Congo and using Bafwali for refueling and an overnight rest for the passengers. This little Airways house had a few bedrooms and a little lounge and bar. When I came into the room there were three people in it—a soiled looking man over in one corner with a bottle of whisky and a glass, a pleasant-looking woman wiping off the bar with a wet rag, and a native boy swatting flies in between periods of falling asleep on his feet.

I liked the woman behind the bar right away because I associated her with the idea of cold beer, and then because she actually produced it. Congo beer isn't bad, and the Airways house had not only a kerosene refrigerator and kerosene, but the wicks to operate with, too. With things all fouled up by the war, they hardly ever managed to get all three of them together at once. The beer was icy cold and I had two bottles and began to have the illusion of getting cooler.

The woman thought I was English, and I let it pass, because I was tired of explaining that I was American and then explaining why I was in the Congo. The place is full of Britishers, but Americans are rare and you get tired of being a novelty.

The woman asked how I liked Bafwali and I told her it was a charming spot.

She laughed and said, "Of course it isn't, but it's nice of you to say so. Do you want another beer?"

I asked her to split my third beer with me and she was pleased as anything. I said, "I thought if there was a native village nearby, I'd go see if I could find some *bilokos*—curios."

"It's three kilometers and no taxi," she said. "Anyway, there's nothing you'd like, just a few ivory carvers, very *indigène*, very native."

I said that was just what I liked, and got into trying to explain that the more successfully the natives imitated European styles the worse their work got, and that their own authentic stuff wasn't crude and ugly, the way it looks to most people, but expressive and so forth and so on, but she couldn't get it. Her own little bar and lounge was decorated with a couple of bad Europeanized ebony carvings of elephants, a celluloid plaque of a pretty girl's profile facing another of a pretty boy's profile, a large plaster cast of a spotted bulldog like the ones we used to get by rolling balls at the state fair, and three pictures: a large brown one of King Léopold and Queen Astrid, a small gray one of the Pope, and a hell of a big bright-colored one of Franklin D. Roosevelt, compliments of the OWI. I looked these over, especially the plaster bulldog, and dropped the discussion of native art, but I still wanted to see what the ivory carvers had to offer. It was hard to find anything really good unless you got into the villages off the roads, but now and then something would turn up in a place like Bafwali. Anything was worth trying so I made her give me directions how to walk to the village.

She gave them to me, but she didn't approve.

"Monsieur will get a *coup-de-bamboo*," she fussed—a light sunstroke that leaves you a little bit daffy.

"Never mind," I said. But she didn't like it. She was shaking her head and worrying as I went out.

I never did get to the village.

I got as far as the post office where I was supposed to turn, and I could see the village a mile or so around the corner, wriggling in the heat, and not a tree in between me and it. There was nobody in sight but a native policeman in blue dungaree shorts and a red fez, standing in front of the post office with his arms folded, staring at me. It was so hot that I began to lose my nerve, and when I looked back in the direction of the Airways house I saw a cloud of dust approaching me, a cloud of dust with a black center that showed up in a minute as a bicycle and rider.

It was the soiled looking man who had been sitting in the corner with the bottle. He came up to me and braked it hard, and stood there holding his bicycle. He smelled of sweat, dust, and whisky, and his shirt was unbuttoned to his waist, showing a scorched chest with some coarse curling hair on it, a few gray ones here and there. He had a long face with a big thin beaked nose that slanted off to one side, and his eyebrows were peaked up in the centers in a theatrical way. He looked around forty or forty-five. With a few minor changes and a little less alcoholic history lined into it, it could have been a good face. As it was, it didn't look like the face of much of a man.

My French was good enough so that I didn't usually have any trouble, but he began talking so fast that I couldn't get what he was saying. But he must have introduced himself because he stuck out his hand and stopped talking and smiled and waited, still smiling. His teeth were stained, but big and strong.

I took the hand and introduced myself. "Hooper Taliaferro," I said. "*Enchanté.*" He claimed he was enchanted too, and called to the policeman. The policeman came over on the double and stood at rigid attention while my bicyclist scolded at

him in Lingala. He was one of those people who always address
a native as if they were ready to rip him to pieces. It seemed to
work but I never could learn to do it. Anyhow this policeman
gave my bicyclist a snappy salute and then turned to me and
gave another, and then about-faced and started off at a jog-trot
down the road to the village.

The man said: "Now that's all arranged, and no *coup-de-
bamboo.*" He was more than half drunk but you could tell he
was used to it. As he talked on I understood him better. The
woman back of the bar had sent him chasing after me and now
I was to go with him to his house and wait while the policeman
rounded up all the ivory carvers and brought them back to us.

He prattled on as we went back the way I had come, past
the Airways house, while he wheeled his bicycle. Yes, I was
right about native art, no, you couldn't find much good stuff
any more. These missionaries (pfui!) burned all the good cere-
monial things they ran across and then perverted native talents
and so forth and so on. It was a pleasure to find someone who
appreciated authentic native stuff, and so on. And he had a
collection at his house that I would really enjoy seeing while
we waited for the ivory carvers.

We walked ten minutes or so before we turned along a
rutty lane up to a small house. It was of rock, and old, only
a couple of rooms long and a couple deep. There had been a
garden but it was waist high in weeds, with a few bushes rising
up and throwing out some common red and yellow flowers.
The rutty lane turned into a short, nicely laid flagstone walk,
also becoming overgrown, up to the front door.

"My home," he said as we reached the step. He gave a
drunken and elaborate gesture. "Enter!" he said, and opened
the door.

I entered, into a small hallway that gave off on either side
into two rooms, both of them with the same dirty floors, stone,
littered with crumpled paper, cigarette butts, some sawdust,
and the short sawed-off ends of boards. There was no furniture, only a lot of wooden boxes nailed shut and piled around at

random. In the room we went into there was a blind, desolate fireplace and overmantel stuck against the wall, one of those despairing suggestions of European life that the Congolese stick into their houses. On the overmantel there was a bottle of whisky, with a dirty glass, a hammer, and a handful of nails. There was nothing else in the room but the miscellaneous trash you'd expect in such a place—an old stained and curling magazine, a broken lamp shade—things like that, lying in corners with the other litter.

My friend crossed over and filled the dirty glass half full of whisky and handed it to me. For himself he picked up the bottle. We sat down on a couple of the packing cases. I was already feeling a little bit uncomfortable because I figured it would take the ivory carvers at least an hour-and-a-half to get there, and if my host got any drunker he was going to be a bore of one kind or another for sure.

He took a long drink from the bottle, and when he threw his head back I noticed the scar under his chin, a couple of inches long, an old scar but a big one, easy to see, slick and white, surrounded by the stubbly growth of whiskers. He set the bottle down. "Now," he said, "we will have an exhibition." He picked up the hammer and went over to one of the boxes.

In a minute he had the top off. I could see the long flat objects rolled in newspaper. He picked one up, unrolled it, and let the paper fall to the floor, and came over to me with the thing supported on the palms of both hands. It was a long swordlike blade about two or three inches wide, curving a little bit and ornamented along its dull edge with a hammered geometrical design. The end of the blade broke into three snakelike prongs, each one writhing to a point. It was a mean looking thing, and a beauty.

"Really *indigène*," he said, "really native, authentic, and old."

He laid it across my lap and began bringing out others. They were museum stuff, some with skin-covered handles and a few with carved ivory ones.

"Beheading swords," he said.

He ripped open another box. This one was full of knives too, but smaller ones. He handed me one in an iguana sheath and I pulled out a blade about eight inches long. But it wasn't the blade, it was the handle that was the wonder. It was just the size to fit a man's fist, and the ivory was so old that it had turned the deep golden brown of strong honey. Most people would have called it ugly, but anybody could have told it was the figure of an adolescent boy. It was all there—the head a little oversized still, the awkward hands and feet, and the bony joints, the shoulders and chest still narrow and flattish. The belly stuck out in a great balloon, the way all native kids' bellies do, and the umbilical hernia that you find in half of them stuck out on top of that. The rudimentary *genitalia* still had the dangling foreskin which is not circumcised until the boy undergoes his initiation into the tribe and official manhood. "Turn it over," he said.

Instead of the reverse of the boy's figure, there was the boy turned into a man. The chest was deeper, the knees weren't knobby any more, the belly had contracted, and there were lumpy muscles in the arms and legs. The whole body was patterned with tiny gashes to represent full tribal tattoo, and now the phallus was grotesquely enlarged over bull-like glands, and prominently circumcised. All the darkness and terror and pride of tribal initiation came to you when you looked at the two figures, the boy turned into a man after a day of torture and celebration. The ivory must have been well over a hundred years old. You thought of the witch doctors who had wielded the knife, and of the hundreds of black boys who had gritted their teeth under it.

"You like that?" the man asked me.

I tried to tell him how much.

"Then take it," he said.

He was drunker than I had thought. The knife was worth money, for one thing, but for another you just don't give away a prize piece from your collection that way. I knew I was going to say I couldn't take it but that I was going to take it if he gave me another chance.

"Take it, take it," he said, waving a hand. "You appreciate these things. Take it back to England and see if your silly English portraits can stand up against it. Go ahead, take it." And it was true; that knife made the Blue Boy look like milk and water.

I put the blade back in the sheath and slipped it under my belt. It was a thrill to know it was mine, and I kept my hand on it.

He ripped open a third box. There was a jumble of odds and ends inside. He pushed around in them until he found what he wanted, then pulled it out roughly so that the things on top of it clattered onto the floor. What he had now was nothing but a big coil of heavy rope.

Nothing, except that when he held it in front of me, proudly, he unrolled it enough to show me the end of it tied in a hangman's knot. "With this I hanged a man," he said. I had the embarrassed feeling you get when somebody tells you stories about themselves that they expect you to believe, and you can't. He showed me how easily the knot slipped back and forth and made me give it a few pushes. "Very fine," I said.

He looked at the rope with enthusiasm. "It was only a native," he said, "but still I can say I hanged a man. Nobody else would do it. Murder is a rare crime among the natives, very rare, and then usually only in the big towns, not in our little places out here. And this was a white man who was murdered—the sub-administrator in M'buku. Not much of a man, not much of an administrator. He wouldn't be, in a hole like M'buku, but after all he was a white man. You've heard of the M'buku rebellion."

I hadn't, but he went on talking as if I had said yes, I knew all about it.

"The other two natives got killed when they captured them," he said, "but this last one was brought back. Of course the administrator here sentenced him to death. It was the first capital crime in Bafwali—the only one. And then nobody wanted to hang him. It had to be a white man but none of them wanted to do it, so I did it."

I believed him now. He tossed the rope across the room onto the box it had come out of. All of a sudden he seemed to lose interest, and he looked tired out. He was haggard at best, but I thought again that it might have been a good face once. He tilted the bottle up and showed the scar again. After a couple of breaths he said, "They paid me one franc to do it. They had to pay something to make it legal. Hangman's fee, one franc. I had the franc made into a watch fob, but I've lost it somewhere."

He started to pour me some more whisky but I hadn't touched what was already in the glass.

"You don't like whisky as much as most Englishmen," he said.

"I'm not English," I said, "I'm American."

"American! What are you doing in the Congo?" There wasn't any secret about it, and I began telling him. He stared at me as I talked, and you'd have thought I was changing form before his eyes. First he looked startled and suspicious, and then it was crazy, but he began to look scared. There was nothing much to what I was telling him, but it certainly meant something more to him than it did to me as I told it, and it made me into somebody he wasn't happy to be around.

I have already said this wasn't a war story and it still isn't. But the Congo was producing a lot of war materials and it could produce a lot more, which was why I was there. Washington had sent a mission of six men to the Congo to serve as liaison with the producers and to see what could be done about increasing production and buying all of it. It was really a simple job because the Congo government backed us up in every-thing we wanted to do. The other five men were working on romantic-sounding things like rubber and diamonds and so on, but I'm a botanist and my particular job was to go to the various stations that were working on agricultural commodities and see how they stacked up. I was classified 2-A and got leave of absence from the University for the job. Maybe you've never heard of pyrethrum or if you have you think it's a garden flower. All the same it has served you well many a time—it's a flower used in making insecticides. Japan grew a lot of it, so after Pearl Harbor we had to find new sources. The Congo had always grown some, and my job was to see what could be done about their growing more and improving the breeds to yield a higher toxic content. Then there were the various fibers that we lost when we lost the Philippines, and the quinine we lost with the East Indies and so on. I was making a tour of the stations to see if I could help out on the plant breeding and to check up on what laboratory equipment they absolutely had to have that we absolutely had to supply. There's nothing obscure or ominous in all that, but I've told you how my hangman reacted to it. "I'm going to Mont Hawa from here," I said.

"Yes," he said, "the government silk-culture station. You'll meet Mr. Rollet there."

"That's the one," I said. Sometimes I thought every white man in the Congo knew every other white man there. "Then Costermansville, to the *Office du Pyrèthre*, and the experimental station at Ineac-Mulungu."

"Mr. Sladden and Mr. Stoffels," he said. "Don't you go to anything but government stations?"

"I go to private ones too," I said. "I'm going to inspect the Congo-Ruzi on this trip."

"I see," he said, and he paused for a long time. Then he said, "I suppose you know who you're going to see there."

"Of course I know," I said. "He has a fancy name—André de l'Andréneau."

It was only a name to me, that I had remembered particularly because it was so fancy, but it went into him like a bullet. He froze there staring at me for a moment, then he broke his eyes away and stood up. "You may wait here for the ivory carvers if you wish, monsieur," he said formally, "but now I must tell you good-by." He didn't even offer his hand, but turned and walked out of the room. I heard the front door close after him.

I certainly wasn't going to run after him to ask what it was all about, and I didn't intend to stay there and wait for the ivory carvers, either. One thing I did know, though. The beers had been doing what beers do, and there was a door in the room which by rights should lead to a bedroom, with the closest imitation to a bathroom that the place afforded. I walked across and opened the bedroom door.

I wished later that I had looked longer, to get a clearer picture of the woman. She gasped and swung quickly around, facing me with her back to the window. With her back to the light that way, all I got was the impression that she was small and young, with heavy dark hair. In the shadow of her face I could see her eyes and mouth—black and red. There was a low bed between us, with crumpled sheets on it. When I tried to remember her that night, lying awake up at the rest house, I found that I could put almost any face on her I wanted to, and it would fit. As for what kind of person she was, my only mental tie-up with her was the rumpled bed, a pretty strong tie-up at that, but one that under the circumstances didn't mean anything. One thing I was sure of: I had discovered something the hangman of Bafwali didn't know, which was that there was a woman in his house that afternoon. She stood perfectly still for the few seconds that I looked at her, then I closed the door and walked back through the house and outside. When I got to the end of the rutty lane there was nothing to see down the road but a little dust. It could have come from a bicycle.

I walked back up the road, and with every step I felt that circumcision knife pressing into my side where I had stuck it under my belt. I kept telling myself it was mine, but by the time I got to the Airways house I knew I couldn't keep it. The fellow had been drunk when he gave it to me, and we hadn't parted friends in any case. I knew it would always be on my conscience if I kept it. I didn't dare pull it out to look at it because I knew that then I'd keep it for sure.

The woman back of the counter was all smiles but I didn't feel like talking pretty.

"The man you sent after me," I said, "will he be back here?"

"Oh, yes, monsieur," she said. She pointed to the table where he had been sitting. "That's his bottle of whisky."

"Then give this to him when he comes in," I said, and pulled the knife and sheath out from my belt and laid them on the counter in front of her.

I tried not to look, but I couldn't help taking a last glance. It was a wonderful piece and I could still have it. "Just give it to him," I repeated, and turned and started out as she picked up the knife. I heard her cry out as she looked at it.

I turned around and said, "What's the matter?"

"Oh, monsieur," she said reproachfully. "So *ugly*!"

She didn't know any English, so I used it to say, "It isn't half as obscene as that goddam plaster bulldog. *Adieu, Madame.*" I never saw her again. But the knife, the hangman, and the woman in his room—that's a different story, or, rather, the rest of this one.

# CHAPTER TWO

## *André de l'Andréneau*

NOTHING HAVING TO DO with this story happened
for the next couple of weeks. I went to the government stations
and made my inspections and they went off well. Everybody
treated me like a prince and I made a lot of recommenda-
tions for equipment because the stations were really doing a
wonderful job. At the end of the two weeks I was tired out and
ready for the few days' rest I had counted on at the Congo-
Ruzi, because my actual work there wouldn't take any time at
all. There really never had been much point in my going there;
it was a tiny station and I didn't see what they could be doing
that the government stations weren't already doing better, but
I had had all these letters from this André de l'Andréneau
asking me to look over the place, so it had been included as a
tag-ender on this leg of my tour. Also, everybody said it was in
one of the most beautiful parts of the Congo. I could already
see that was so, if it was anything like Costermansville where I
wound up the last of the government stations. Costermansville
is on Lake Kivu, five thousand feet up, and the mountains go

up another five or seven thousand from the edge of the water—
great disorganized looking mountains thrown around without
any reference to reasonable geology.

It turned out that I had company, not entirely welcome,
for my trip from Costermansville to the Congo-Ruzi, a ten-
hour drive that I had looked forward to doing alone. The
Congo agricultural commission had turned over a little pickup
truck to me for my inspections, and they insisted that I go on
and use it for the trip to the Congo-Ruzi too. They didn't have
to insist very hard because there wasn't any other way to get
there except to ride the *poste*, the mail truck that made the trip
once a week on a strictly God-willing basis.

The Kivu country was wonderful, all volcanoes and
strawberries. I had never seen a volcano nor had my fill of
strawberries and I got fixed up on both deals. It's fabulously
green country, everything from blackish blue-greens on up
through the sickish yellow-green of the banana patches. The
natives grow these patches everywhere for making banana
beer, which is what they live for. It's a thick brownish slush
with bubbly scum all over the top, smelling like a cross between
chocolate and paint remover, and liberally spiced with the
carcasses of drowned flies.

I drove along through this country wondering about
André de l'Andréneau. When my hangman walked out on
me in Bafwali I had my first suspicion that there was something wrong with the Congo-Ruzi and especially with de
l'Andréneau. Nobody else ever walked out on me, but every
time I mentioned de l'Andréneau's name, people would start
hiding behind their faces and talking about something else. I
reread the letters I had had from him but they were only the
usual European business letter, full of a lot of highfalutin stock
phrases.

It took about half an hour to get into country that looked as
if no white man had ever been there before except for the road,
which turned into a miracle of hairpin turns. I had to cross a
barrier of mountains and when I went down the other side it got

hotter and hotter, and big open patches, brown and dry, began to appear in the green bush. Sometimes they would be burned black from grass fires. The dust got bad and there was no air stirring, so that sometimes I would go down around a hairpin turn and come back into my own dust settling from above.

So I hated to pass this White Father on his motorcycle. He was kicking up a pretty good dust-cloud himself, skittering over the loose surface of the road at a good clip. He was a particularly fine specimen complete with sun helmet, and I could see the points of his long beard flying back over his shoulders. When I honked at him he drew over to one side of the road and stopped to let me by, straddling his motorcycle. I couldn't bring myself to pass him up so I drew alongside and asked if he wanted a ride. It took him about ten seconds to tuck his white robe up around his waist and sling the motorcycle into the back of the truck before I could get out and help him. He was a sturdy guy, like all these Fathers out there.

I kept telling myself that I was in a very interesting situation, riding through the wilds of Africa with a picturesque man of God, but it didn't help much because Father Justinien turned out to be just a plain bore. He was smiling and affable all the time, but that was part of the trouble. I don't know just how old he was. There was plenty of salt and pepper in his beard but not many lines in his face.

He couldn't get over the idea that any American could come to Africa for anything except to take movies of it or write a book about it, and he kept saying to me, "*Ça mérite quelques lignes, ça mérite quelques lignes,*" all the time, he was so afraid I wouldn't notice every mountain. He was right about the landscape meriting a few lines. It was wonderful, but every time we turned a corner, which was every few minutes, I had to burst into new cries of admiration and astonishment, or Father Justinien would start goading me into it.

There was nothing on the road between Costermansville and the Congo-Ruzi except two little gas and emergency stations. Father Justinien was going all the way to the last of these, called Ruzi-Busendi, so this ride was a break for him. I had just finished one of my required appreciation routines when I saw another big curve coming up, so I said to Father Justinien desperately, just to have something to say, "Do you know a man named André de l'Andréneau?" He did. He gave a start and the smile came off his face and he forgot about the scenery.

"I'm on my way to see de l'Andréneau," he said.

"You mean you're going on to the Congo-Ruzi station?" I asked. It wasn't so surprising after all; there were only two or three places he could be going on this road. "So am I. You won't have to get off at Ruzi-Busendi, you've got a ride all the way."

He said, "Thank God," not rhetorically, but as if I had really been sent along in the Lord's work. "We may be in time yet."

"What do you mean, in time?" I asked.

"But you know about de l'Andréneau?"

"I guess I don't," I said.

"He's dying," said Father Justinien. "He may already be dead. I had a letter on the *poste* from Madame Boutegourde asking me to come. I think it must be her idea—she's a Godly woman, very Godly, and de l'Andréneau is far from a Godly man, very far. Although he may have felt the need of the church when he felt the end coming. Some of them do. You must know Madame Boutegourde?"

"I don't know any of them," I said, and told him why I was going to the Congo-Ruzi. "This really knocks things into a cocked hat as far as my inspection goes," I said.

Father Justinien looked uneasy at that, so I said, "There's no point in my going now but I'll take you there anyway. You'd be two days on your motorcycle."

According to Father Justinien, André de l'Andréneau needed extreme unction just about as badly as anybody could need it. I began forcing the truck, and Father Justinien began talking less. I discovered that if I took the turns fast enough he lost interest in the scenery and concentrated everything on hanging onto his seat. I got a new picture of myself, rather pleasant, as a heavenly messenger in a race against the forces of evil, a sort of angel of deliverance in a pick-up truck. From then on things were quieter and we made good time.

At Ruzi-Busendi they had put out lanterns to stop us. We saw the lights from away down the road, and then as we got nearer we saw them lift up in the air a few feet and begin waving from side to side. There were four or five of them, and when we drew up to a stop the native boys drew close to the truck holding the lanterns high. Their eyes glistened and the light slithered over their oily black skins.

A middle-aged white woman came hurrying toward us from the little building at the roadside. She came up to the window on my side and said, "I beg your pardon for stopping you, monsieur, but have you seen—" but just then she caught sight of Father Justinien and broke off. "Oh, there you are, Father!" she cried.

"This young man picked me up on the road," said Father Justinien. "Madame Boutegourde, this is Mr. Taliaferro. He is the young man who is going to make an inspection of the station."

"Oh, the American!" said Madame Boutegourde. "*Enchantée, monsieur.* We tried to reach you. Have you told him about André, Father?"

"I can go back, and make my inspection some other time," I said. "I wanted to get Father Justinien here."

"Oh, no," said Madame Boutegourde. "You must stay now, we will find places for everybody."

I could see only her face and shoulders in the lamplight, and one hand resting on the window of the truck cab. She was forty-odd with very fine dark eyes and dark hair drawn back from her face. Except for the eyes her face was undistinguished and a little plump with middle-aged plumpness, but it was pleasant and intelligent looking. The hand on the door was small, with the skin a bit reddened and shiny. She had good fingers with the nails cut short, and she wore a wide gold wedding band.

"I have a truck here," she said. "If you will follow me now."

As she turned and walked away I caught a glimpse of the rest of her. She was a little taller than average and considerably plumper, but she looked strong and solid, not flabby, and she walked erect and with a vigorous stride as she disappeared into the dark.

To one side of the road the lights of the station truck went on and we saw Madame Boutegourde lean out of the right window and motion us to follow. Apparently somebody else was in the driver's seat—a native boy, I saw later. The boys with the lanterns piled themselves into the back of Madame Boutegourde's truck and we started off.

As soon as we turned off the road onto the Congo-Ruzi's lane, we began to jounce and bump. The boys in the truck ahead had to cling to the sides, and I thought they would break their lanterns. In a general way we were going uphill again, but I had come down a lot from Costermansville during the day, and now it was only beginning to cool off a little bit.

"Madame Boutegourde is a very fine woman," Father Justinien told me between jounces. "She and Monsieur Boutegourde have been in the Congo for twenty years now; they are real Congolese. Madame Boutegourde will cook you a real Congo meal." He let his voice grow roguish and said, "*And* they have a very pretty daughter." I was too tired to make a roguish response so I let it pass, and after half an hour the truck ahead stopped and Madame Boutegourde came back to us. I could see lights a few hundred feet off the road. "If you will come with me, monsieur," she said. "Father, if you will wait in my truck—unless you want to see Henri?" Father Justinien said he would see Debuc tomorrow, and climbed out. We said good night and Madame Boutegourde climbed in beside me.

She directed me down a side lane toward the lights and after a minute or two I could see a small open-looking house surrounded by a flimsy porch. All along the porch against the light were the silhouettes of plants trailing out of hanging baskets.

"I'm being a lot of nuisance at a time like this," I apologized.

"No, no," she said. "We are only sorry your visit will be less pleasant for you. It is very good of you to come. My husband looks forward so much to talking to someone from America. This is Henri Debuc's house, a young man your own age, monsieur."

Henri Debuc was already out on his rickety front steps as we drew up in the truck and stopped behind a rusty Ford. The headlights raked the man long enough for me to see that he was big. He came on down the steps and I saw he moved with a kind of slouching grace.

"Henri," said Madame Boutegourde, "I am taking you by surprise. This is our American, Mr. Taliaferro, who came after all. With Mademoiselle Finney at Gérôme's, and Mademoiselle Collins at our house, and Father Justinien in the guest house—"

"Of course," said Debuc. He smiled noncommittally and we shook hands. His sleeves were rolled up and I saw a heavy, loosely muscled arm that was a fit with his broad athletic build. He had a wide full mouth and a short broad nose, and pleasant blue eyes under brows that were so light they showed whitish against his ruddy face. There was only one thing I wanted more than to fall into bed, and that was to have a nightcap before I did it, and I discovered that I liked the idea of having a drink with Henri Debuc. There was a bottle of whisky in my bag. I began to feel better.

Madame Boutegourde had forgotten she would have to get back to the road, so I had to drive her back in the truck. I said good night to her and again to Father Justinien, glad to see the last of him for the day. When I got back and parked the truck and went up the front steps, ready to propose the drink, Debuc was just bringing out his own whisky and a couple of glasses.

"I'll show you your bed in a minute," he said, "but you'll want this first."

Henri Debuc had that kind of big, easy-going, full-bodied and round-muscled good looks that runs to belly and jowls in middle age. But Henri wasn't middle-aged, he wasn't more than thirty, and I envied him the effortlessness of his attraction. He wasn't "magnetic" or any of those words. In fact he was a little bit slovenly, but every movement he made suggested a kind of lumbering vitality that was sexual as all hell. His habitual expression was a kind of half smile, without any particular gaiety to it. The first thing I always wonder about new people is what they manage to do for a living and how they arrange their sex life, because it seems to me that those two activities plus sleep and a movie or two account for most people's twenty-four hours a day. You felt about Henri that normally he would live in a routine indulgence of his good healthy viscera—eating, mild drinking, and plenty of women, never having to hunt too hard for his opportunities and never feeling anything much one way or another about them the next morning, or at any rate not anything that couldn't be expressed by a good stretch, a shower, and break-fast. But this wasn't Europe, it was the Congo-Ruzi, and as usual it turned out I was wrong, because Henri's life had included something like youthful idealism, real personal tragedy, and a disillusion that his easy-going half smile never suggested. I wondered what kind of life a man like Henri managed to lead at a tiny station where everybody was under everybody else's nose all the time. There were always the native women, but that's low stuff and unsatisfying, without the eating and drinking and dancing and companionship that make the rest of it worth while. Anyway the Belgians don't go in much for that kind of thing. The British colonials accept it as a substitute and the French think it's rather fun and the Portuguese are crazy

about it, but the Belgians avoid it both as a matter of prefer-
ence and colonial policy.

Henri was wrong about me, too, because he regarded me
as a kind of exotic personality, when God knows nobody is less
exotic than I am when I'm at home. Of course when you come
down to it I was exotic in the strict definition of the word, so
much so that as I guess I've already said, I got tired of being
a novelty. I was doubly a foreigner, because any white man is
a foreigner in equatorial Africa, and I was a foreigner among
the Belgians too. Somehow you always think of the other
fellow as the foreigner even when you're in his country. I was
always surprised to remember that I was one, and by the time
I reached the Congo-Ruzi, tired out from my other inspections
and from driving the truck all day, I had developed a pretty
authentic case of homesickness. I suppose that was why I stayed
up with Henri that night and got a little bit drunk instead of
going to bed, tired as I was. Because I felt with Henri just the
opposite of the way I had felt with Father Justinien. I felt at
ease. I even felt almost at home in Henri's house, somehow.

It was a crazy dilapidated place, of a type they used to
build a lot in the Congo before bricks and concrete were easy
to get. It was a precarious skeleton of thin iron pipes perched
five or six feet off the ground on stone stilts. The walls and
floors were nothing but thin wooden partitions hanging to the
iron, and here and there they were rotted through, or chan-
neled with ant runs. The curtains at the windows and doors
had been bright native prints but now they were faded and out
of shape. All around the house there was the rickety veranda,
with all these hanging baskets and plants trailing out of them.
The plants were orchids, but Congo orchids aren't much, with
their tiny inconspicuous blooms.

The thing that made it like home to me in spite of all of
this bizarre stuff was that Henri or somebody had furnished
it with a few clean, spare, usable pieces of furniture and a
few pieces of native art, all good. There were some beautiful carved canoe paddles crossed on the wall, some black

pottery with spouts in the shape of human heads, and one little ancient fetish, ivory, even darker than the handle of that circumcision knife. It was of a man clutching his abdomen in both hands, and had probably been carried as protection against dysentery and the whole list of intestinal ailments that ravage the natives. Finally on the walls there were half a dozen small oils of quiet landscapes and simple interiors, typically amateur as far as technique was concerned, but with a nicer feeling for their subject matter than you usually find. Henri said these had been painted by his brother, a dentist in Antwerp.

So the thing that made it like home to me, a little bit, was the spareness and selectivity that I had known all my life in the houses of students and professors. It didn't fit in at all with my first impression of Henri and was my first hint that I was going to have to revise my opinion of him.

Among other things over the first couple of drinks, Henri told me about the other people at the station, but since they all come into the story I'll tell about them as they show up. Over the third drink I began to hint around to see if I could find out what it was about André de l'Andréneau that was so fishy. Henri countered with a question of his own.

"Why didn't André want you to come here?" he asked suddenly.

"He did want me to come here," I said. "I had the most cordial letters from him."

"I know those letters," said Henri. "I wrote them myself for André's signature. I mean later. He was all right when we sent the letters, but a couple of weeks ago, just about the time he got sick, he asked Gérôme to wire your offices not to send you." Gérôme was André's elder brother.

"I didn't get the wire," I said.

"Gérôme didn't send it. He may have led André to think he did, but Gérôme was too anxious for you to make the inspection. I suppose you know you're going to be the life or death of the Congo-Ruzi?"

THE DEVIL IN THE BUSH 25

I didn't like that because my premonitions weren't so good, so I changed the subject. I told him how much I liked the room we were in and why it made me think of home, of the University.

"I'm glad you like it," he said. "Your life at your University sounds good. It can't be anything like this, really. Life would be hell here if I didn't find ways to make it painless. I can't make it enjoyable, the way César Boutegourde can, but I can keep it from hurting."

"You could always leave."

"No, I came out on a five-year contract."

"How long ago?" I asked.

"Nearly five years," he laughed. "Yes, I could leave. I could leave the fifteenth of next month. In fact it looks very much as if I'll have to. I suppose now that André's in the shape he is they'll keep me on a little longer, but I'm in a good way to be fired." He took a swallow of his drink. "And a good thing for me, too," he added.

"That's crazy," I said. "You've got a doctorate from Louvain."

"It's a good degree and I used to be a good botanist," he admitted, "but I've done a rotten job here. I'm not even sure I could get a job at another station. I could have had my pick five years ago if I hadn't signed for the Congo-Ruzi in Belgium. I didn't know what I was getting into; it sounded good and they offered more than the government stations. But that was five years ago and the Company has been folding up ever since. I'd have left before I went to seed, if I hadn't signed that long contract. If they fire me now I'll take any old job, and glad of it. Do you mind all this getting so confessional?"

"I like it."

"I'd better let up. You might put it in your report."

"What's your particular recipe for making it painless?" I asked.

"Oh, a lot of semiprofessional fiddle-faddle. The orchids, for one thing. And these." He set his drink down and swung lazily around in his chair to lift the lid of a neat painted chest next the wall. It was full of birds, gutted and dried with the legs folded up against the slit bellies. The feathers were in perfect condition, glossy and shiny where they were supposed to be, still soft and downy in other places. The reds had gone a little brown but they always will, no matter how good you are at specimen work. Henri pulled them out of their paper tubes one by one, and laid them on the table. Some of them were flashy and iridescent; others were soft gray-white with rose colored tips to the wings and cherry-colored beaks. The feathers still felt alive.

"It's taken a lot of time to find all these," I said. "Is this why you've done a poor job—spending your time on other things?"

"If I hadn't done this I'd have sat twiddling my thumbs," he said. "I've got a lot of others. Do you think you could get them past customs for me? I've thought I might sell them in America."

Everybody was always asking me to do things like this.

"Maybe I could," I said, but I couldn't put much enthusiasm into it.

"The hell with it," said Henri. "I'm flat broke and just happened to think I might sell them. Forget it."

"What in the world do you find to spend money on out here, to be flat broke?"

"There was a little thing called the invasion of Belgium," Henri said. "Most of my salary checks had been deposited there. And lately the good old Congo-Ruzi has been paying me in stock."

We began putting the birds back in their tubes and into the box.

"I've got a little more than dried birds to show for my five years," Henri said. "Tomorrow morning you'll drink the best cup of coffee in the Congo. I grew the beans and dried them and roasted them, and tomorrow I'll grind them and drip your coffee."

"Look," I said, "you're a good man and you really enjoy this kind of work. Why have you done such a poor job—if you have."

"I have, all right," he insisted. "You're here to make an investigation—"

"No, an inspection," I said.

"Amounts to the same thing," Henri said. "If I tell you why I've done a poor job I'll have to violate professional ethics and also speak ill of the dead. Have we had enough drinks for that?" He smiled to show it wasn't as serious as it sounded.

"I think we have."

He didn't smile when he said, "I've done a rotten job because nobody could have done a good job under André de l'Andréneau." He stopped.

"Go on," I said. "What was the matter with him?"

"Among other things he was an incompetent drunk," said Henri. "I keep saying 'was'. It'll do, though. He's in the past tense now, all right—not a chance to recover. I must be getting drunk myself. It's fun to talk so much. It's like being in college again. I think I know what you mean when you say this room makes you think of college. I can see it now. What was I saying?"

"André de l'Andréneau was an incompetent drunk."

"I could go on a long way from there," Henri said. "He was an incompetent drunk. He was also a very poor businessman. That's no moral defect but it's been damn hard on the Congo-Ruzi. Also he was a seducer, a fornicator, a nigger-beater—worse, too, I think, but that's all I know. I imagine other things. I'm sorry I said all this."

"Forget it," I said.

"*You* forget it," said Henri. "Let's go outside. I'll show you my garden."

He had laid out a crisscross of gravel paths with a circle in the middle. In the pale light I could see a few sturdy garden flowers—cosmos, gaillardia, common day lilies, a few dahlias. In the middle, in the circle, there was a topless oil drum on a pebbled cement pedestal. There was a hole cut in one side of the drum, with a pane of glass sealed into it. "It's for fish," said Henri, "but they die as soon as I get them in there. Too hot. Look over here."

It was a wire cage with a thatched roof, about eight feet high and as far across. Henri lit a match and held it up. I could barely make out a black crested eagle on his perch. "Tomorrow I'll make him scream for you," said Henri.

"Here's a lady I want you to meet."

Flanking the eagle's cage on the other side of the little garden there was a miniature native hut not more than three feet high, in the center of an enclosure made by a miniature bamboo stockade.

We stepped over the stockade and Henri lit another match and went to the door of the hut, bending down to look in. "Come, Dodo," he said. The match went out but he had awakened Dodo, and she came staggering out into the moonlight on sleepy legs. She was a mouse antelope, only about eighteen inches high to the top of her head, mostly legs and as soft as a kitten. She came out to us and nuzzled at Henri's shin. We squatted down and when Henri pushed Dodo over to me she came without hesitation, and thrust her nose between my knees and up into my ribs.

"She's almost grown," Henri said. "She won't get much bigger. I found her in the bush when she was really little. You know it's funny about the antelopes. When they made the Albert National Park the antelopes were protected from the natives and most of the animals that prey on them. And instead of increasing they began to die out. They don't breed unless they're preyed upon."

"Dodo's got a nice home and won't be preyed upon," I said. I picked her up in my arms and she lay there as gently as a house pet.

"Some night something will come out of the bush and get her," said Henri. "Maybe another animal, maybe a native. Poor Dodo! But they all die that way anyhow. I'm feeling better. Let's go in."

I put Dodo down and when I looked back at her from the steps she was still standing at the little stockade.

"I'm tired," I said. "I think we'd better go to bed."

"You're using my bed and I'm using the couch in the other room," said Henri. "Don't fuss about it because it won't do any good." I made the mistake of drinking what was left in my glass as we passed through the living room. We went into the bedroom and undid the mosquito net and Henri began taking off the sheets. I made helping motions.

"I talked a lot," said Henri. "There's one thing you never did answer. Then I'll be more circumspect. Why didn't André want you to come here?"

"I haven't got an idea in the world," I said. "Maybe it was because his station is in such lousy shape. It's a sorry way to be welcomed, though."

"André never cared about the station," Henri said. "He used to laugh about how embarrassed you'd be to see how bad it is. It was Gérôme and Boutegourde who wanted you to come. Something happened. He had some personal reason." The last part of my drink was busy being just that much too much. I began to have agreeable feelings of being abused.

"I think it's a *hell* of a way to be welcomed," I said, feeling sorry for myself because I was so homesick again. "Me a foreigner and all. He didn't even want to see me."

"Well, you'll never see each other now," said Henri. "Let me finish these sheets myself."

He did, while I began undressing. He went out and came back after a minute with some aspirin. He poured a glass of water from a carafe by the bedside and made me take two pills.

"What's André de l'Andréneau got?" I asked.

"Amoebic dysentery," said Henri. "The worst kind. Good night, Taliaferro."

"You call me Hoop," I said. "I'll call you Henri. G'nigh', Henri."

"All right, good night Hoop," said Henri, and went out. I wasn't really tight but I was a little bit dizzy. I lay there and it didn't take me long to go to sleep, but the last thing I thought of, of all things, wasn't anything to do with the Congo.

I kept thinking of Yvonne Printemps in a show I had seen in Paris in 1937, *Trois Valses*, where she did a little tap dance in black velvet slacks and sang a song, *Je ne suis pas ce que je semble*. It had a catchy little tune but I could only remember the first line. It kept going through my head and I kept seeing her dancing. She didn't tap very well but she got away with it by dancing as if she were letting the audience in on the little secret that she wasn't really very good at it. She held her arms out to the sides and did this little tap step, back and forth, back and forth. *"Je ne suis pas ce que je semble,"* I heard her singing over and over again—"I am not what I seem, I am not what I seem, I am not what I seem." She was still singing it when I went to sleep, a long way from home.

It was as close to prophetic vision as I ever expect to come. There was hardly a person at the Congo-Ruzi who wasn't trying to fool me one way or another, and most of them got away with it.

I woke next morning with someone tugging at the sheet. The air was cool, and the pale lemon-colored sunlight came through the window in a long slant, so I knew it was early, not much after six. Henri was on the other side of the mosquito netting.

"André died during the night," he said. "The funeral's at seven-thirty. We'll have to hurry."

I didn't see why I should go to the funeral of a man I had never seen, but Henri was taking it so for granted that I didn't say anything. He went out and I managed to pull myself out of bed.

A houseboy came in with a pitcher of wash water and a towel and some soap. He took a lot of time setting these out ostentatiously just so, then he turned and spread out his face in a big smile. It showed filed teeth in a face covered with spectacular tattoo. The purplish lozenge-shaped welts spread out in concentric circles on his cheeks and fanned up across his forehead from the bridge of his nose.

"*Moi-je 'pel Albert*," he said in his own version of the French language. His name certainly hadn't been Albert before the missionaries got hold of him; with teeth and tattooing like that he hadn't been born in the bosom of the Christian church. He was in it now, though, and he had saints' medals to prove it, hanging on a string around his neck with his own heathen jujus. When it comes to religion the natives always play both ends against the middle.

Albert had a fine broad chest and shoulders, and bulging pectorals. His torso knotted itself down into compact hips and his belly looked like cast black metal, but like all native bellies it arched outward and spoiled what would otherwise have been a beautifully slung together body.

"Glad to know you, Albert," I said. "*Je 'pel Monsieur Taliaferro.*"

He gave me some more of his jibber-jabber but I couldn't understand it this time. I stood and smiled at him, which I had learned was the technique. He made the same jabber again, but this time he pointed to the pitcher with one hand and made the motion of drinking with the other. Then he shook his head in a violent negative and bent over clutching his belly in a spasm of agony. Then he straightened up and grinned and pointed away from the pitcher to the stoppered carafe by the bedside and went through the whole rigmarole again, except that this time he was just as violently affirmative and rubbed his belly in ecstasy. He was a wonderful pantomimist and I enjoyed the show, but if there's any time you don't have to be reminded not to drink your wash water, it's when you're about to use it to shave with so that you can go to the funeral of a man who has just died of amoebic dysentery.

"All right, Albert," I said. "O.K. to drink out of the carafe."

Albert cackled in delight. "Ho-kai, ho-kai!" he said, happy as a kid, and went out of the room. We were getting along fine.

Through the doorway I saw him pick up the ivory fetish and rub it a couple of times over his belly.

I got shaved and dressed and went out onto the veranda. Henri was waiting for me at a shaky table with a clean white cloth on it. I sat down and unfolded my clean white napkin that had holes worn in it. It was still cool and it was pleasant out there. Somebody had soaked the orchid baskets and they dripped with little cool noises.

"Sorry to hear about de l'Andréneau," I said.

"Sorry to have to wake you to go to a funeral," said Henri. "It's good of you to go. This funeral—you've no idea what a poor thing a white man's burial can be out here. Just a raw hole in the earth with a wooden box if he's lucky like André, and half a dozen white men to see him off. Then too you represent the American government and André was head of the station. It may sound funny to you, but it makes it a much better funeral, your being here."

"Anything I can do to help," I said, trying to sound less stiff than he did. His manner was self-conscious and I saw he was suffering from the feeling you get the next day, after you've jumped the gun a little bit in sharing confidences or intimacies. I'd seen it lots of times, the morning after drunks had cried all over me and told me about their love life and so on. Henri hadn't told me very much, but the Belgians expect any friendship to stay on a formal basis longer than Americans do. All the same it made me feel disappointed and let down.

The coffee was really good, but when I told Henri so he said, "I'm glad you like it," almost coldly, and I gave up. We had to hurry anyway and it was a good excuse for not talking, and for not finishing Albert's reasonable facsimile of toast, soaked in canned butter that tasted of preservative and wax. Albert had given it to me with a big happy smile and the proud announcement that it was "toas' 'merican," and I began to feel that he was the only friend I had in the Congo.

When we went down the steps and across the little garden to Henri's car I added Dodo to my list, making two. She came stepping delicately out of her hut and followed us as far as she could along the stockade, and the last I saw of her she was watching us bump along the lane to meet the other cars. I decided right then that I wouldn't stay out my four days at the Congo-Ruzi. I didn't like it there. I would spend that day and the next, and then go back up in Costermansville for a couple of days until my plane got there. Also it would eliminate the chance of missing my plane if the truck broke down on the road going back.

They had chosen an open unused field about two miles from the center of the station to bury André de l'Andréneau. It sloped down to a deep valley, and across the valley there were the turbulent green mountains you saw everywhere around there, with the brown patches blackening and giving off smoke as the grass fires crept across them.

The station truck was pretty far gone, like everything else at the Congo-Ruzi. It led the line down the road, with four native boys in clean white shorts holding the coffin in place as the truck jounced over the ruts. I caught a glimpse of Madame Boutegourde in the car just ahead of us. There was another car between her and the truck-hearse, and Henri and I brought up the rear. The sun was on us now and we began to choke on the dust, and to sweat, that early in the morning. When we reached the field everybody got out of the cars and stood while the natives took the coffin on their shoulders and started across the field to the grave. The hole was raw enough. The fresh up-turned earth was bright red against the chemical greens of the bush beyond. Along the edge of the bush you could see here and there the crooked bleached-looking branch of a fever tree with its vermilion pom-poms and no leaves at all.

The coffin was an awkward box made of lumber from knocked-down packing cases. If he had been the Governor General and died out there, de l'Andréneau couldn't have done any better. There's a twenty-four hour burial law in the Congo, and the sooner you get it over with the better, because there's no embalming even in the big towns, and once you're dead you don't last long in that climate. André was lucky to have this box at all. Lumber was one of the tightest items on the whole colony list because you couldn't get the mechanical saw blades for cutting it since the war. I know that Papa Boutegourde didn't feel any grief for André de l'Andréneau that morning, but he could have wept when that lumber went down, because it was some he had been hoarding for his new seed beds.

I was never able to think of César Boutegourde as anything but Papa. He just looked like it. He and his wife and a young girl were ahead of Henri and me as we all straggled across the field after the coffin. The boys set their load down by the grave and withdrew to a respectful distance while the white people came to uncertain stops in their own isolated groups. The Boutegourdes stood some twenty feet away from me. To look at them they might have been Respectability Triumphant, the mayor and his wife and daughter in any prosperous Flemish town. They made the exotic landscape look out of place behind them instead of looking out of place against it. The banana groves and the fever trees became offenses against normalcy.

Papa Boutegourde held his sun helmet in his hand while his bald head and his spectacles shone in the morning light. Madame Boutegourde managed to nod to me with an ambiguous expression that did what it could to combine friendly recognition of our meeting the night before with the proper funereal reverence of this morning. She was the only person there who had made an attempt at mourning. The threadbare black skirt and black waist were unbecoming, and without the lanterns to make them shine, her eyes weren't as fine as they had been when I first saw her.

The girl with the Boutegourdes looked eighteen or nineteen. She was nearly as tall as her mother, and while there was nothing fragile about her she was nicely trimmed down in the right places—the ankles, the waist, the wrists, the throat. She had on an honest simple white dress that would have been just clothes anywhere else but was really good for that part of the world. She had white shoes but no stockings and her legs were tanned, which was unusual for the Congo, where a pale skin is still fashionable. The dress was cut to fit tight from the waist up, and across the front it confined the girl's high swelling breasts in a way that made me uncomfortable. I was looking at them when I raised my eyes and found her looking at me. She had a calm face with exceptionally regular features, pretty and fresh, with a lock or two of light sun-bleached hair escaping underneath the white hat. She knew what I had been looking at but she let our eyes meet curiously for a moment before she turned hers slowly away, without embarrassment. This was Gabrielle Boutegourde, the pretty daughter Father Justinien had told me about. I remember that what I thought most about her that first morning was that she had a beautiful healthy girl's figure and I kept feeling uncomfortable because her dress was so tight across the front that I felt as if I couldn't draw a full breath. And I thought that for a young girl stuck off in the Congo she had unusual poise. She and Madame Boutegourde stood in the same easy, erect and graceful attitude, and it occurred to me that some day Gabrielle's figure would achieve the pleasant monumentality of her mother's.

I didn't expect wailing, or people throwing themselves over the coffin at this funeral, but no one there showed any signs of having so much as been under a strain. We stood as patiently as cows in four little groups, very small in the violent landscape. My shirt was already sticking to my back. Father Justinien and the coffin made up one group. He looked as sturdy and sensible and unspiritual as Papa Boutegourde as he stood there reading the service, but he read it with deliberation and reverence in spite of his heavy robes and the increasing heat.

The Boutegourdes made their own group, and Henri and myself ours. There was a fourth group of three people who stood under a tree near Father Justinien in the only spot of shade in the field—a man and two women. The man had rather long hair with a wave in it, a toothbrush mustache, and a handsomely near-aquiline nose in a ruddy face. I'd have taken him to be British if I hadn't known he was Gérôme de l'Andréneau, André's brother. His chin projected strongly without giving him an air of force, and his perfectly arched brows had an artificial symmetry. He was tall and should have been good-looking, but there was something about him that suggested the good looks of a man who has depended on his face and figure to get him by—like a matinee idol without talent. I couldn't believe that I could have seen him before, but I had the feeling that I knew his face. That happens lots of times and I tried to dismiss it, but there it was. I kept wondering.

The two women made incongruous companions for him in their serviceable dun-colored cotton dresses, like a couple of gunny sacks tied in the middle. One of the women was slightly built and looked mousy and sweetish, but the other one I'd have trusted to get me out of a tight spot anywhere, if she were my friend, and I'd have hated to have her working against me. She stood straight and strong with her freckled arms and big hands across her stomach. Her hair was hidden, but from her freckles I knew what it would be—coarse and carroty. Both the women had on old sun helmets freshened with thick coats of shoe whiting, and I'd have guessed them to be about the same age as the man—around forty-five or even fifty.

Father Justinien came to the end of a phrase and turned his eyes to the man and the two women. They began to move from the shade toward the coffin. Papa and Madame Boutegourde exchanged a look and a slight nod, and began to move forward too, with Gabrielle following. Father Justinien lifted the top half of the coffin lid, and I found myself being pushed along by Henri in the wake of the Boutegourdes, and realized that we were all going to have to file past the coffin for a last look at André de l'Andréneau. So I was going to see him after all.

I watched them as they went by ahead of me.

The tall elegant man was first. He stopped by his brother's coffin and glanced down. Nothing changed in his expression. As he looked up our eyes met for a fraction of a second. I was certain I knew that face, and my vague memory of it was mixed up with some feeling of dislike. He walked back into the shade and stood there quietly, avoiding my eye.

The mousy woman crept up to the coffin next, sighed dutifully as she looked in, and walked away. She was the only person there who felt obliged to put on a little act.

The carroty-haired woman with the freckled arms paused longer. She stood there as if she were really saying good-by. She stayed quietly looking down at de l'Andréneau for a long minute with a nostalgic and reflective expression on her strong, plain face. Then she walked on and joined the tall man and the other woman under the tree.

Papa Boutegourde walked up quickly, looked in so shortly as to give the impression of rudeness, and walked off. Madame Boutegourde did as Madame Boutegourde would: she simply walked up, she simply looked in, and she simply walked away again and stationed herself beside Papa Boutegourde. Gabrielle was just in front of me. It was a matter of six or seven steps to the coffin. I know that she took the last step with her eyes closed. Then she averted her head quickly to open her eyes and walk away.

I felt self-conscious as I walked up myself. I knew they were all looking at me, and I wondered if I could look interested without looking curious, and respectful without looking indifferent or pious. I should have been worrying instead about looking surprised and staying there too long. I stayed even longer than the carroty-haired woman. I had seen André de l'Andréneau before.

There had been no undertaker to fix him up, so he had none of that false air of hypnotic sleep of an embalmed corpse, but I recognized him. The face was more tired and wasted, but it was the same face—the peaked eyebrows, the hawk nose crooked to one side, even the stubble on the chin, because they hadn't shaved him. It was my hangman of Bafwali. His head was thrown back stiffly and the chin jutted up, showing the slick white scar along its underside. And now I knew why the tall man under the tree looked so familiar. His regular features were those of his dead brother, straightened and unravaged.

So I didn't get to see how Henri looked into the coffin. It took everything I had to walk naturally out into the field a dozen paces and wait for Henri there. I didn't dare look at anyone. I knew that this ought to explain everything that happened in Bafwali but I couldn't patch the pieces together. I could see why everybody avoided comment on André de l'Andréneau but I had seen that last night. They hadn't anything good to say of him, so they didn't say anything at all. I can look back now and see what a puny little puzzle it was, and as a matter of fact I got that part of it straightened out very soon after. It took me longer to discover what one of the people standing there in the field already knew, and what another suspected—that André de l'Andréneau had been murdered; and when I did find it out, it was already too late to save another of us from being killed.

Right then all I wanted to know was what had happened to make de l'Andréneau hide his identity from me in Bafwali and later on try to keep me away from the station. I looked at the people standing there while the boys sweated at lowering the coffin into the red earth, and I felt shut away from them. The only faces that were anything but impassive were those of the natives, contorted with the strain of letting the ropes out slowly as the box went down.

"I am not what I seem—I am not what I seem—I am not what I seem." Later on, the woman with the carroty hair elaborated on the same idea, and I might as well put in here what she said to me:

"I try to be as honest as I can," she told me, "but when it comes to other people out here I always look twice. It seems to me that everybody in this part of the world is two people—not always Jekyll and Hyde stuff, either. Sometimes two kinds of Jekylls, and as often as not two separate kinds of Hydes. People change when they come out here. They go on acting the same to hide the change, or they make up a new character for themselves to keep laid over the change, but whatever they do you'll find more false faces per capita among white men along the equator than you could find scare-faces if you searched every witch doctor's hut in the Congo. There's some kind of devil out here in the bush that changes people. Maybe the real stuff inside them gets a chance to come out the way it wouldn't in real white man's country, just the way a lot of people get to feeling away from everything and lose their inhibitions on shipboard, and act different from the way they act at home. Or maybe they really do change. Anyhow I always look twice, once on top and a good long time underneath. And you'd better watch out," she added to wind it up, "because it can happen to you, too." It did happen to me in a small way, which brings me to me and Gabrielle Boutegourde.

# CHAPTER THREE

## Gabrielle

AFTER THE FUNERAL I was introduced to Gérôme
de l'Andréneau and the two women. Gérôme said he was sorry
that he couldn't see me that day, but that I would understand.
He would see me tomorrow and we would make the inspection and talk things over, if that was convenient for me. He
knew I would enjoy dinner at the Boutegourdes that night,
and if I needed anything that he could help me with during
the day, please call on him, and in the meanwhile Henri would
take care of me. I said I'd be happy to spend that day doing
nothing at all for a change, and tomorrow for the inspection
would be fine.

When Henri and I got back to the station, Henri said he
had to spend the morning in the laboratory unless there was
something he could help me with. Whether this was true or
whether he just wanted to get away from me I wasn't sure, but I
said that was fine, I'd just fool around his house and get a little
rest. So I dropped him at the laboratory and drove his car on
down to the house. I said hello to Dodo, who gave the impres-

sion of nodding a greeting in her fragile and ladylike way, but the eagle fixed me with a malevolent yellow eye and hissed slightly through his beak.

I went into the bedroom and undressed and got into my pajamas and lay down for a cigarette. After that I thought I'd like to read. There were no books in the bedroom so I went into the little living room, although I didn't remember seeing any there either. I was right—no books. It was out of character with that otherwise homelike room. I wandered out onto the veranda and walked around it until I found Albert hanging some laundry on bushes in a sunny stretch back of the house. When he saw me he grinned and came running up to the veranda. He said to me, "Toas'? Toas'?"

"No thanks, Albert, no more toast," I said. "I want a book." He didn't understand my French any better than I understood his, so we went into the house together and I pulled out of my suitcase an *Oxford Book of English Verse* that somebody had thought would be just the thing for me to carry around the Congo. "*Livre, livre*," I said.

He brightened and cackled and said, "*Liv', liv'!*" Then his face fell and he spread his hands wide and said something like "*Boolay, boolay.*"

I gave up the French and told him, "I don't get it," in English.

He went into one of his pantomimes. His eyes darted around the room until he saw my box of matches on the bedside table with my cigarettes. He grabbed the box and opened it and pulled out a match, and pantomimed lighting it. He walked over to me, giving a wonderful imitation of a man protecting the flame of a match, and then very carefully he bent over and went through the motions of touching the flame to the *Oxford Book of English Verse*.

"*Liv' boolay, toot boolay*," he said, and straightened up to see if I'd got it this time.

"*Livres brûlés!*" I cried out. "Books burnt—all the books burnt?"

He gave that delighted cackle again and began showing me how a big fire had been built. He made the motions of throwing book after book into the fire, and finally he dug a hole and buried the ashes.

I felt goose flesh popping out on me at the thought of books being burnt alive; and out there, where you needed books so much and they were so hard to get, the burning had the scary quality of pointless violence.

I made the motions of throwing books on the fire myself, and asked Albert, "*Monsieur Henri?*"

"*Oui-oui,*" he said. "*Monsieur Henri,*" and he became for a moment Henri, throwing books onto the fire and watching them burn.

I went in to lie down for another cigarette. The goosefleshy feeling went away and a completely puzzled one took its place. I lay there watching the cigarette smoke curl and drift in the heavy air. Then after a while I went to sleep. I woke up for lunch feeling logy, and it wasn't much help dousing my head in the washbasin of tepid water. We had a good lunch, fresh tomatoes and canned corned beef. Henri seemed more communicative but now I had my own reasons for feeling standoffish.

"What would you like to do this afternoon?" he asked. "There are some boiling springs nearby—if you like boiling springs. That's just about all, within an afternoon's reach."

"I think I'll just lie around some more," I said. "I can take an awful lot of sleep. Do you suppose I could find a book somewhere?"

"The Boutegourdes have a lot of standard stuff—classics and that kind of thing," he said, without batting an eyelash. "Gérôme might have something livelier. Shall I go ask him for something?"

"I'd enjoy going myself," I said. "How will you spend the afternoon?"

"If you really don't want to do anything special I'll put in some more token time at the lab," he said, and after lunch he told me how to get to Gérôme's and left.

All the houses on the place were within a few minutes' walk of one another but isolated by differences in level and clumps of thinned-out bush. It took me maybe ten minutes to walk to Gérôme's. The grounds of the station were naturally beautiful in spite of being badly kept up. There were lackadaisical natives around about, listlessly making a show of sickling grass or chopping undergrowth. Gérôme's house was an awkward cement structure that had been painted a sort of yellow color, now mostly chipped or washed off. But the house was solid and the living room looked comfortable enough in an ungainly way. Gérôme let me into it with a surprised polite smile, running his fingers through his uncombed hair, so that I thought I must have caught him lying down. We made a little polite talk for a while but nothing we said amounted to anything except one thing:

"I'd like to borrow a book, if you have one you can lend me," I said.

"Of course," said Gérôme. "Take any you want." He showed me his three or four dozen books lined up between book ends. "But if you couldn't find anything at Henri's, I'm afraid you won't want any of mine. He's got a much better collection."

I picked out a book of chit-chat about Paris celebrities called *Gens du théâtre que j'ai connu* by a kind of French gossip columnist, and when I got back to Henri's I undressed again and lay down and read for a while. I couldn't keep my mind on it and I went to sleep again, until Albert woke me up to take a bath and get dressed for dinner at the Boutegourdes'.

The Boutegourdes' house was what you would expect—like Gérôme's but smaller and uglier. When Henri and I got there the cell-like living room was already crowded with the three Boutegourdes, the mousy woman, and the freckled carroty-haired woman, and too much big heavy furniture that was just as bad as what the Boutegourdes would have had back in Belgium. There was an overpowering display of spears and arrows on one wall, but Madame Boutegourde made Papa keep his devil masks and fetishes hidden away. The mousy woman was a New Englander—Miss Emily Collins, missionary, from Milford, Connecticut, a long time ago. The red-headed one was Miss Mary Finney, M.D., medical missionary, born in Fort Scott, Kansas, in 1892. They had a regular itinerary that they covered in a broken-down station wagon. They had been here ever since André had been taken sick, so that Miss Finney could take care of him, but ordinarily they would show up at the Congo-Ruzi for two or three days every couple of months on their regular rounds. Miss Finney would doctor and Miss Collins would take care of the spiritual needs of the natives by teaching them to sing hymns like *Will There Be Any Stars in my Crown, in my Crown,* translated into Lingala and accompanied by six drums. Henri was a dawdler, and by the time we got to the Boutegourdes' everybody had highballs except little Miss Collins and Gabrielle, who had glasses of pineapple wine. We came to the door and Miss Finney was waving her glass around and saying to Papa Boutegourde, "My God, César, I don't see how you can say it. You saw him as well as I did, lying there with his throat cut from ear to ear and half the flesh stripped off his back." As we came in the door she glanced over and said, "Oh, h'lo Henri, h'lo Mr. Taliaferro," and then went on scolding Papa Boutegourde. "If it wasn't for my medical oath," she said, "I wouldn't touch another of your goddam M'bukus with a ten-foot hypodermic. You're crazy." Madame Boutegourde greeted us and showed us a couple of chairs in a hostessy manner. Gabrielle smiled and nodded and Papa Boutegourde fetched a couple of highballs for us and there was the rigmarole of becoming part of the group. When we got settled I said, "Don't let us interrupt you, Miss Finney. What's a goddam M'buku?"

"Have I been swearing again?" asked Miss Finney.

"You know you have, Mary Finney," said Miss Collins.

"Every time I swear, Emily busts into tears," said Miss Finney.

"I do not," said Emily.

"You do too," said Miss Finney, and Miss Collins gave it up. Henri stepped into the breach. "Albert's a M'buku," he said. "They're the leading tribe around here. Miss Finney hasn't much to say for them."

"They're the meanest blacks in the Congo, I'll say that much for them," Miss Finney told him.

"But Albert doesn't strike me as being mean," I said. "I like him." I felt sorry for Miss Collins, who was fiddling nervously with the hem of her skirt and looking pretty well squashed. She had a pallid, grainy face with light brown eyes and scanty hair crimped in some kind of patent waver. I said to her, "Miss Collins, do you approve of the way Albert wears his saints' medals and his jujus on the same string?"

"Well," she answered me, "I always say you have to meet the natives half way. Especially these M'bukus." She was sitting on the edge of a low chair with her knees pressed together and her feet apart and pigeon-toed. She kept pulling her skirt down tight around her knees. "Anyway," she added, "Albert doesn't wear his jujus for *religious* reasons. He wears them for *medical* reasons."

"Oh, for crying out loud, Emily," said Miss Finney. "Why don't you just give up and admit you can't do anything with Albert?" She turned to me. "Emily's the soul-snatcher in this outfit," she said, "and I'm the doctor. We represent the body and the spirit between us. God knows why we haven't killed each other during the last twenty-five years, but we haven't."

"I don't give up and admit anything of the kind," said Miss Collins. "Albert's been a very faithful boy."

Miss Finney grunted.

"He's been a very syphilitic boy," she said. "You needn't worry, though, Henri—I gave him that examination this morning and you just keep on giving him the injections." Henri nodded; all that evening he just sat and watched the rest of us, relaxed in his chair and looking as if he enjoyed it, but saying hardly anything at all.

Miss Collins coughed daintily and nervously, took the tiniest sip of her drink, set it down on the table by her side, and pulled at her hem.

"Emily," said Miss Finney, "if you pull that damn skirt one more time you're going to have it right down off your neck. After the things we've done the last twenty-five years I should think you could take a little reference to syphilis without fidgeting. You've got a chronic case of New England girlhood, that's what you've got." She added as an afterthought: "I'd rather have syphilis."

Miss Collins coughed again and glanced meaningfully at Gabrielle.

"Oh, that," said Miss Finney. All this had been in English. She said in French, "Gaby, did you understand what we were saying?"

Gabrielle said in English, "Not very much of it." She had a very strong and very delightful accent. She was wearing what I thought must be the same dress she had worn at the funeral, but she had added a pretty bunch of bright cloth flowers at one shoulder and a bright soft belt. And tonight the dress didn't fit too tight across the front. Her breasts stood out beneath the cloth and you could see them beginning to swell where the neckline was cut. I looked at them as little as I could, but it was hard to keep from it.

"You may like Albert," said Miss Finney, "but you better be careful how you let an arm or leg hang out from under the mosquito net. He's only one generation removed from cannibalism. His tribe used to hunt pygmies the way they hunted antelopes, and for the same reason, too."

"No," said Papa Boutegourde. "Not for the same reason. For sport, not for food. No human being ever ate another because he tasted good."

"Oh, I know, I know," interrupted Miss Finney.

Somehow all the words she used sounded abrupt and rude, but she spoke with such an air of honest good humor that the effect was warm and friendly. "They eat each other because the eater will absorb the desirable qualities of the eaten. They used to make sterile M'buku women eat parts of pygmy women because pygmy women are fertile as rabbits. Well, you can have my share."

"Really, Mary," breathed Miss Collins, but I looked at Gabrielle and she was smiling at them.

Miss Finney said, "César, you ever eat stewed pygmy? You've eaten everything else."

"Not quite everything," said Papa Boutegourde modestly. His eyes lit up behind his spectacles and Madame Boutegourde looked apprehensive. "Grasshoppers, yes—and caterpillars and monkey and snake," he said, "but not everything. Not that piece of elephant's trunk. I tried, I tried very hard," he said, and Madame Boutegourde began to look as if her worst fears were about to be realized, "but it was too much for me. It was cut into round pieces like Bologna sausage and fried. It would have been all right, but for those two little holes in each piece. No, they were too much, those two—"

"César!" wailed Madame Boutegourde. "Not before my dinner!"

Miss Collins choked on her wine and set it down quickly while she groped for her handkerchief. She got hold of herself and said, "Never mind me," and sat there fanning herself.

"No, for goodness sake never mind, Emily," said Miss Finney. "You haven't heard anything yet. Mr. Taliaferro, you ever hear of the M'buku rebellion?"

"Only the name," I said. "Wasn't it around Bafwali?"

Papa Boutegourde looked puzzled. "What gave you that idea?" he said. "No, it was on one of our own plantations, only forty miles from here—our own little rebellion."

"I wouldn't be proud of it, César," said Madame Boutegourde.

Miss Finney said, "It's a fine bloody story. Let me tell Mr. Taliaferro. *I* never minded what happened to Duclerc, nasty little thing. You see, Mr. Taliaferro—oh, for goodness sake, what's your first name?"

"Hooper."

"Well, this nasty little Duclerc was subadministrator and after the natives had worked out their road-tax—they all pay a road-tax in labor—he kept them working on his own planta-tion, and no pay."

"And a gun and whip to back him up, remember that," said Papa Boutegourde.

"All right, a gun and whip to back him up. I guess there was a lot to be said for the natives," admitted Miss Finney. "But he made his mistake when he hired a couple of Kitusis to stand guard."

Papa Boutegourde interrupted. "The Kitusis had always warred on the M'bukus," he said, sounding like a classroom lecturer all of a sudden, "but even in the old days, the M'bukus hadn't eaten Kitusi flesh because they regarded the Kitusis as their inferiors. However, when Duclerc hired—"

"*I* started this," Miss Finney broke in. "I know you know everything about native history and customs, César, but I'm trying to get to the bloody part. Hoopie's a tourist."

Papa Boutegourde shrugged and settled down to his drink.

"*Well*," said Miss Finney with a certain relish, "it was the most excitement this place ever saw. Three M'bukus got the Kitusis, then they went on and got Duclerc. Damn fool, if he hadn't hired the Kitusis he'd have got away with it. White men are still sort of demigods out here, but not when they play with Kitusis. They dragged Duclerc out of his house into the bush and cut his throat and took three strips of flesh off the back of his shoulders. I *suppose*," she said, "they cut his throat first. I know they ate the flesh."

Madame Boutegourde moaned faintly. "My dinner," she murmured.

"That's all," said Miss Finney. "It's a nice story for tourists and happens to be true into the bargain. They got one of the M'bukus alive and hanged him right there on the plantation."

I wondered why André de l'Andréneau had told me about the hanging but claimed it was in Bafwali. But I only asked, "Who hanged him?"

Papa Boutegourde said, "They asked me to, but I couldn't bring myself to it. Monsieur de l'Andréneau volunteered."

Madame Boutegourde said miserably, "Does anybody here still feel able to eat my dinner? I have palm-oil chop."

You could eat palm-oil chop at the foot of the gallows and enjoy it. It's the tough Congo chicken stewed into melting tenderness in palm oil, red peppers, and its own juice, then garnished with crystallized lemon peel, candied chestnuts, ripe olives, cinnamon sticks, pickled peaches, and anything else you can think of.

I took Gabrielle into the dining room, and Madame Boutegourde had put us together on one side of the table, with Henri between Miss Finney and Miss Collins on the other.

"It's a very pretty dress," I said to Gabrielle as we sat down.

"I am very happy if you like it," she said. "It's the same one I had on this morning. I only added the flowers and the belt." Everyone was making sit-down conversation with somebody else. For a moment Gabrielle and I were talking to one another with nobody else in on it. She said: "And I let it out some, too." She looked at me with a little smile and added, "—as I think you have noticed."

She took me so by surprise that I stammered like a fool. She didn't look like the kind of girl who would be giving you a lead, but at the same time it hadn't sounded like a rebuke. She turned her eyes away from me in a manner that was a dismissal, and picked up her napkin. As she unfolded it in her lap she smiled at Henri across the table.

"It's so nice to have you here again, Henri," she said. "How is Dodo?"

She kept that same calm manner all through dinner, but I noticed something else. Under the shield of the table she would clench her napkin or twist it in her fingers. Then she would stop, but before long she would be at it again, her hands twisting and clenching until the napkin was moist and crumpled all over.

The next morning Henri took me to the building that served as administration center and laboratory for the station.

Gérôme de l'Andréneau was late and Henri went back to the laboratory to get it in order. Gabrielle was at a desk back of a typewriter, and handed me a letter that she said the *poste* had brought on its trip back from Costermansville. It was a long letter of instructions from Tommy Slattery, who was head of our mission in Léopoldville. I saw it was mostly routine stuff, but at the end there was a page scribbled in Tommy's own hand, so I stopped to read it:

P.S.—The 4th of July blowout was a great success. Everybody came, even the Governor General. Somebody brought along a Madame de l'Andréneau who has just blown into town. *Hod—ziggady!* Bad timing, Hoop, you there and her here. T.

P.S. again. Later. You may see her after all. She's going back to the Congo-Ruzi because of somebody's sickness or something. The hod-ziggady still goes. Don't forget you work here.

Tommy Slattery had an infallible instinct when it came to what he always called the hod-ziggadies, but my taste didn't always agree with his, so the only thing I knew for sure about this Madame de l'Andréneau was that Tommy's instinct told him she was pretty easily available.

I folded the letter and slipped it into my pocket, and said to Gabrielle:

"I didn't know you worked here."

"I help out," she said. The morning was still fresh and pleasant and Gabrielle was a perfect part of it. She wasn't working yet—just sitting, with a breeze coming in the window and blowing her hair a little bit.

"Gabrielle," I said, "you're an awfully pretty girl."

"I am very happy if—" she began, but she knocked it off and finished up with just a "Thanks."

"What shall I call you?" she asked. "You have such a funny name."

"Hoop," I said.

"'Oop," she repeated. "That's funny too!"

"The way you say it it is," I said, "but I like it."

"I shall call you 'Oop. Sit down." She patted the desk top beside her, and I went over and sat down on it.

"Gabrielle—" I said.

"Gaby, most people say."

"I don't like it. It makes me think of Gaby Deslys or somebody like that, not you. I like Gabrielle."

"Gabrielle, then. What were you going to say?"

"I was going to say that if this were America, I'd ask you to go to a movie or to a dance somewhere."

"Oh, I wish we could!" she cried out. "This place—!" She checked herself and went on in her calm way, "Girls must have a wonderful time in America. They're all beautiful and they have lovely legs and beautiful clothes and they do as they please."

She had lovely legs herself. "What can we do here?" I asked her. "Something we don't have to do with everybody else."

"Nothing," she said.

"Then we haven't a chance for a date?" I didn't know a French word for "date" so I used the English one.

"Date? What's that, date?"

When I explained to her she said, "No wonder we don't have a word for it. We don't even have it. Mama or Papa would have to come along, even if we were engaged."

"Well," I said, "what can we do about it?"

"Nothing," she said, "not a thing."

"That's too bad."

"Very too bad," said Gabrielle. "I would like so much to have just one date."

She got up and took a step to the window and stood looking out. Outside the window there was a beautiful blue sky with mounds of pearly clouds; there were mountains; there was a gaudy fever tree hung with its crazy flowers. "Here comes Gérôme," she said.

She turned and faced me, with her back to the window, so the light was behind her. I remembered a woman in a mussy bedroom in Bafwali, but it couldn't have been Gabrielle. She wasn't smiling any more and she said, "If I could have just one date like an American girl! You know, 'Oop—how would Mademoiselle Finney say it?" She groped for a minute and then said in English, with her wonderful accent, "Miss Finney would say this is a 'ell of a place, 'Oop. 'Oop, it is. It is one 'ell of a place, one 'ell of a place."

Sweetness on the desert air, I thought. But I had a question to ask.

"Before Gérôme gets here," I said, "is there a Madame de l'Andréneau?"

"Why yes—Jacqueline."

"I mean what is she," I asked, "mother, wife, widow, or what?"

"Gérôme's wife," said Gabrielle. "What makes you ask about her? She's in—oh, maybe you met her, in Léopoldville. She'll be back here any day now, I guess—do you like her a lot?"

"I don't even know her," I said.

"Then why are you so curious about her?"

"I'm not so curious about her."

"You ask questions about her."

"I only want to know what she's like," I said.

Gabrielle opened her mouth, but just then Gérôme came through the door. I said to Gabrielle, "Sorry about the date."

"A 'ell of a place," she whispered, and then aloud, "*Bon jour, Gérôme.*"

❀ ❀ ❀

Gérôme, Henri, and Papa Boutegourde took me all over the station that morning. What I thought of it can best be summed up by part of a letter I wrote back to Tommy Slattery:

*Dear Tommy,*

*I feel in a spot, but there's nothing to do about it. These people are so nice to me that it's going to be heartbreaking to* turn in the report I'll have to turn in. Remains of a flourishing station everywhere you look but in no condition worth our while to rebuild. Monsieur Boutegourde does whatever is done around here. He showed me his new seed-beds (for pyrethrum marriages, if that means anything to you) which are very good as far as they go but completely inadequate for the job. There's an old grove of cinchona trees that could have been the basis of a quinine program if the original plans, begun about fifteen years ago, had been carried through—but like everything else here, it's gone to pot. They've been working hard on pyrethrum since the price went up but they've only met average production standards.

It's a shame because the place could be so good. Management has been just plain rotten or nonexistent. The laboratory technician and general assistant, Henri Debuc, seems like a nice fellow but for some reason he has laid down on the job after getting off to a good start five years ago.

Most of this decay is the fault of André de l'Andréneau, that we had the correspondence with. I got here to find him just dead—amoebic dysentery, and I hope you're having the lettuce washed in permanganate as I told you. Two years ago his brother Gérôme came up here to see if he could save anything from the wreck of the company. Seems they had plantations all around Bafwali too, but lost them, and Gérôme came up here to try to get this area's concessions into working order as well as to get the experimental side of the station into something like operation. Gérôme is head of the whole shebang; André was director of the station and more or less of the concessions in this district. The plantation owners are dropping out as fast as they can get rid of their contracts. In short, the Congo-Ruzi is on the skids.

I'll write this into a formal report later but I thought I'd let you have the word. I got your letter— including the P.S's. I've decided to leave here in the morning so unless she gets here today I'll miss your Madame Hod-Ziggady. (She's Gérôme's wife.) The way you talk she sounds like Dr. Slattery's

*Favorite Remedy. She'll have to be really something to shade out a very sweet number named Gabrielle who is up here wasting her sweetness on the desert air, but this one is strictly a nice kid, although I know your theory about all women over the age of fourteen.*

It took most of the morning to go all around the station. When we got back, Miss Finney was waiting in the office with Gabrielle.

"Henri," she said, "where's my culture on André?"

"Do you mean to say you want to see that thing again?" asked Henri. "It's right there in the laboratory."

"With a hundred others, it is. I can't find it in all that mess you've got."

Henri said, "I'll show it to you, but you know it's amoebic."

"Sure I know it's amoebic, but I want to see it all the same," Miss Finney said. "I like to look at it. You got anything else interesting?"

"Not much," said Henri. "That ear fungus smear you brought in is ready, if you think that would be fun too."

"Henri's wonderful," Miss Finney said to me. "He can do anything. He makes all these cultures and everything and he's got some wonderful slides. If only we had a better microscope. Henri, you ever get sections of that tumor I brought in?"

"If Henri can 'do anything,'" said Papa Boutegourde abruptly, "it's too bad he does nothing."

Henri only smiled. "If you don't need me, Gérôme," he said, "I'll take Miss Finney into the laboratory."

"I excuse myself also," said Papa Boutegourde. "I am sorry, Monsieur Taliaferro, that we hadn't better to show you." I hadn't said anything, but Papa Boutegourde wasn't fooling himself, and he was in a bad mood.

"Gabrielle," he said, "are you coming now?"

"I want to finish a little something," Gabrielle said, although there wasn't anything in the typewriter. "I'll come along soon."

Papa Boutegourde said good-by and went out, and Gérôme and I went into his office and closed the door. Just before I went in I looked at Gabrielle. She looked at me like the cat that swallowed the canary, and I knew she was waiting there to tell me something.

Gérôme de l'Andréneau lowered himself elegantly into the chair behind his desk, and began fooling with a pencil, turning it end over end slowly, watching it. He pursed his lips slightly as he watched the pencil, and his toothbrush mustache bristled out. Then he sighed and laid the pencil down with a sharp click, and said to me:

"Well, Mr. Taliaferro, that is our little station. I am afraid I am not happy over what you probably think of it."

"There's no point in stalling," I said to him. "Our programs are emergency ones and you're not in a position to get under way, even with the help we could give you."

"No," said Gérôme, "I am afraid we are not."

He picked up the pencil again and concentrated on it, following it with his eyes as he turned it in slow somersaults. There wasn't any reason for me to, but I felt like a dog. "Of course," I said, "if I find we have anything to spare that would help you, there's a bare chance we might work in the Congo-Ruzi on one of our programs—perhaps the pyrethrum. But everything's awfully tight—"

He laid the pencil down again and looked at me waveringly and said, "No, no, Mr. Taliaferro, if we are lost, we are lost. The Congo-Ruzi has been shrinking for years now. I came out here to save what was left, but I had had too little experience with it in Belgium. I lived off it only. Of course my brother André—but the less said about that the better. It wasn't until our father died that I began to take the thing seriously."

"But this business of the emergency program doesn't mean the life or death of the Congo-Ruzi Company," I said.

"Not exactly," said Gérôme. "We can go on as a very small company but I'll have to spend the rest of my life out here keeping it running. I can never afford to hire a manager and go back to Belgium to live on the income as I used to do. I had only hoped against hope that we might get in on the new programs. Well," he said, forcing a cheery smile, "that is not your trouble and we will stop talking about it. In the meanwhile we enjoy your visit here."

I told him why I thought I had better leave the next morning.

"Oh, no," he said. "Madame de l'Andréneau will be here tomorrow or the next day. If I let an American go before she gets here she'll never forgive me. America is such a magic word. Poor Jacqueline, she was sure everything was going to be again the way it was in the old days when we were making money."

"I'm sorry about it."

"It isn't your fault. Will you and Henri have dinner with me tonight? The rest will be there too."

I accepted for both of us and got up to go. He stood up too and pulled out his watch to look at it. The fob was made of a Congo one-franc piece.

"Hello," I said, "what's that on your fob?"

"A souvenir," he said, and handed the watch to me. "Perhaps a rather grim souvenir. As a matter of fact, it was my fee for hanging a man. One franc."

I guess I looked surprised enough.

"Only a native," he said, "but still, I can say I have hanged a man. They paid me this one franc to make it legal."

"Oh, yes," I said, "the M'buku rebellion. They were talking about it last night at the Boutegourdes'." I tried to remember. They had said that Monsieur de l'Andréneau had done the hanging, they hadn't said André or Gérôme.

"Then you know all about it," he said. "I came up here because the subadministrator was on one of our plantations. All the officials balked at the job, and—well, I did it for them."

I handed the watch back to him and he looked at it with obvious pleasure for a moment, and then dropped it back into his pocket.

"You could have taken some of the rope and had it reworked into a fob-strap," I hinted.

"That's true," he said, pleased at the idea. "I still have the rope. Jacqueline wouldn't let me keep it in the house. It's in Bafwali—I gave it to André to store with the other things in our house there. I have a good collection of knives, but Jacqueline won't let me keep them in the house either. Do you like this one?"

He pulled open the drawer and took out my circumcision knife. It was even better than I had remembered it.

I went through the routine of examining and admiring it. I handed it back to him and said, "Well—"

"Good-by for now, then," said Gérôme. "Until tonight." I was so busy trying to figure it all out that I passed right by Gabrielle at her desk in the outer office.

"'Oop!" she called.

I went over to the desk.

"What's new?" I asked.

"Did you ask me for a date?"

"I said I would if I could. Can I? I do, now. How about a date?"

"Of course," she said. You never saw such a pretty smile.

"When can you make it?" I asked.

"Why, tonight, of course!" she said.

"But I've got to have dinner with Gérôme. How—"

"Me too," said Gabrielle. "Afterwards. After we are through with dinner."

"Golly," I said. "You pick up American ways fast. That's a late date."

"Late date," she repeated experimentally. "Here, take this." It was an envelope.

"Don't open it now," she said. "And don't let Henri see it. He's still in the laboratory with Miss Finney. I don't want Henri to know anything about it. Or anybody. Now go away." Outside I paused to rip open the envelope. She had penciled a little map of the station, with an X, at one spot, and little arrows showing how to get there.

I stuck my head back in the door.

"How do I get rid of Henri?" I asked.

"You'll just have to do something about him," she said. "I can't take care of everything."

I decided not to wait for Henri to get through in the laboratory with Miss Finney, so I started out on the way back to his house alone. I walked along mulling it over in my head and I began to see what had happened in Bafwali. That is, if Gérôme really was the hangman.

When the bicyclist had first come up to me he had babbled along in French that was hard for me to understand, and then had stuck out his hand for me to shake. I suppose he had introduced himself and I had missed his name. And when I told him mine, he got only the pronunciation "Tolliver" instead of whatever he had been making out of "Taliaferro" in my letters. Then he had thrown this cock-and-bull story at me about the hanging and so on, even using the same phrases that Gérôme used when he told it. When he had already glamorized himself by taking credit for the whole adventure, he discovered who I was and that I was going to show up at the Congo-Ruzi station where I would meet Gérôme even if he, André, managed to wiggle out of seeing me. The hanging story was bound to come up, and he hadn't any idea how to wiggle out of it. He would look pretty silly. He was willing to sacrifice the possibility of government help for the Congo-Ruzi in order to save himself some trivial embarrassment, so he had tried to keep me from coming for my inspection.

I heard a whistle and somebody running behind me. It was Henri. I waited and he caught up with me, panting a little bit.

"Finish with Miss Finney?" I asked.

"She's crazy," Henri said. We began walking along together. "She wanted to see that culture on André again. Then she kept going over all my old slides, that she knows by heart already, and asking all kinds of questions about them."

"She's a nice person," I said. "I like her. She makes an odd combination with Miss Collins, though."

"Don't underestimate Emily Collins," Henri said. "She may look like a mouse but she's got the determination of a mad water buffalo."

"Miss Finney wouldn't have stuck with her all this time if she weren't some kind of real person," I said. "Oh—Gérôme wants us for dinner."

He stopped in his tracks and turned to me. "*Me?*" he said.

"Sure. He just now told me to tell you."

"Well I'll be damned." Henri laughed. "You're a great asset to my social life. I haven't had my foot inside Gérôme's door for nearly two years."

"I'm not asking any questions," I said. "The way you shut up on me yesterday morning, I'm not taking any more chances."

"I talked too much that first night," he said, "but anybody would tell you about this. I don't get along with Gérôme's wife. It's the damnedest thing. On a tiny station like this one, people have to watch their dinner lists as if it were diplomatic Lisbon. If Jacqueline's going somewhere they have to see that I don't get there, and vice versa and so on. It doesn't make for easy living, but on the other hand it gives us something to do."

"What's the matter between you two?" I asked.

He spread his hands in a gesture of ignorance. "I'd answer that too, if I could," he said. "It's just that Jacqueline won't have me around. I like her well enough. We got along fine when she first came here—saw a lot of each other, and I went to their house a lot. I swear I didn't give her any reason to, but all of a sudden she froze up and—I don't know what it was. She's never offered any explanation, at least not any that has ever reached me. But she's certainly unrelenting, whatever it is. Hardly speaks to me when I do see her by accident."

"What's she like?"

"Oh, she's small, very good figure. I don't suppose you would think she's pretty. She's not pretty in the American way. She's about thirty-five. Very French. She's French, not Belgian, that's one reason I don't think you'll think she's pretty. She was an understudy or something like that in the *Comédie Française* when she married Gérôme. That was only seven or eight years ago. I guess—" He stopped.

"Go on, what do you guess?"

"I guess she decided she'd never make the grade. She was twenty-eight by then. So she got married. She was lucky to get Gérôme, a man with plenty of money, at that time, and a good family too, and willing to marry her. She'd had lovers, not casual affairs but a series of protectors or whatever you want to call them, and normally she'd have gone on and made a career of it the way the rest of them do, but Gérôme fell for her. He's really crazy about her. It looked like security and money for the rest of her life."

"Does everybody know about this?" I asked him. "Madame Boutegourde seems so conventional, I should think there'd be some conflict there."

"Of course everybody knows it or I wouldn't be telling you," he said. "I suppose Angélique Boutegourde would turn on Jacqueline and tear her to pieces, if Jacqueline were down. But Jacqueline's not down—she's up as far as the Boutegourdes are concerned; she's the boss's wife. Here we are."

We turned down the road that led to Henri's house. I could see the corner of the garden with the eagle's cage.

"You never did make that eagle scream for me," I said.

"We'll do it now, if Albert has a piece of raw meat," said Henri.

"I'm not changing the subject," I said. "Go on about Jacqueline."

"Oh. I said she was up, as far as the Boutegourdes are concerned. But as far as she herself is concerned, she took an awful tumble. Her type doesn't really care for anything except pretty clothes and attention from men, and when the Congo-

Ruzi began to go down-hill, Gérôme pulled her out of Europe for this place. They thought it was going to be for only a few months while he made a checkup, and I suppose Jacqueline pictured herself on safari the way they do it in the movies—nail polish and all. Well, they're stuck here now, first because they haven't got enough money to go back, and second because of the war. Jacqueline's sunk pretty low when Léopoldville looks like heaven to her. That's where she is now, I suppose you know."

"She's coming back any day now," I said.

"Is she? I'd never be told." I wasn't as sure he took it as indifferently as he was acting.

"Another thing I wanted to ask you," I said, "while you're feeling communicative. Did Gérôme really do that hanging?"

"Of course," said Henri in real surprise. "I was there. What makes you ask that?"

"It seems a little out of character, that's all. He's a nice guy, but you wouldn't think he'd have the guts to go around hanging people."

"Sure," said Henri, "he's indecisive and temperamental. I like Gérôme too, and I admire the show of courage he's making in trying to pull the Congo-Ruzi together, but he's coddled himself too long."

"Then how could he hang a man?" I asked. "Nobody else was willing to, but he did. Doesn't that show some kind of strength?"

"Not necessarily," said Henri. "Maybe some kind of weakness. It's a simple thing to spring a gallows trap. Somebody else rigs it up, ties the knot, sticks the guy's head into it and everything, and all Gérôme had to do was stand there and knock out a wooden pin with a hammer that somebody handed him. If you wanted to prove to yourself and other people that you were really quite a man, that would look like an easy way to do it. No danger, no nothing. If you were selfish enough, and weak enough, and eager enough to prove you were strong, what easier way than to spring the trap under a poor black nigger that somebody else had condemned to die anyhow? It wasn't something Gérôme *had* that made him willing to hang the fellow when nobody else wanted to. It was something he lacked." Henri had been speaking irritably, almost angrily. He paused a minute and then said, "I guess I'm just a sorehead."

"You're all right," I said. "There's nothing wrong with you that a woman and a change of scene wouldn't cure."

"Is that all?" said Henri, and I realized that I had named the two things that were most impossible in his situation. But an image of Gabrielle popped into my head. I had asked him enough. I didn't ask him why propinquity and all the other factors in favor of it hadn't thrown him and Gabrielle into the marriage bed long ago.

We turned into the little garden.

"Well," said Henri, "I've always got Dodo. She loves me even if Jacqueline doesn't." The little antelope was nuzzling at the stockade, and we both reached over to give her a scratching back of the ears. She snuffled with appreciation and made little punching motions against the stockade with the end of her nose, but when we went up the steps onto the veranda she turned away and started cropping at a little pile of carrots and lettuce leaves in her feedbox.

Albert came out, grinning as usual. He had the table all set on the veranda, and he began jabbering away to Henri in his outlandish tongue. All I could catch was that it was about Father Justinien.

Henri turned to me and said, "You're moving. Father Justinien cleared out this morning and they're putting you in the guest house. Albert wants to know if he can pack your bag. What he really wants is a legitimate excuse to look over your things."

"I don't mind," I said. "But I don't want to move out—except that you can have your bed back." And then it occurred to me too that I wouldn't have to do any finagling to get away from Henri to Gabrielle that night.

"You'll be more comfortable over there," Henri said. "You'll have a couple of boys to heat your bath and so on. I'll tell Albert to take your things over there while we're at dinner tonight, on his way back to the village."

"Ask him about the raw meat too," I said.

Albert produced a strip of meat and when we went out and Henri held it up near the wire netting, the eagle raised its crest and gave a series of raucous screams that sounded as if they must be tearing his throat to pieces. Then Henri threw the meat between the wires onto the dust of the bottom of the cage. The eagle pounced on it and held it down with his yellow claws while he ripped into it with his beak. He gulped it down with painful jerking contortions of his neck.

"I gave him a live rabbit once," Henri said. He stood and watched the eagle tearing at the meat. His eyes stayed fixed on the bird until the last strip disappeared. The eagle waddled about on the bottom of the cage while the spasmic jerkings of its neck subsided. Henri gave a slight shudder and turned to me.

"He was eating at it before he killed it," he added, and we went in and sat down to a lunch I had lost my appetite for.

Even if there hadn't been Madame Boutegourde's wonderful dinner the night before for contrast, Gérôme's would have been bad anywhere. It was an imitation of a good European meal, but it had only one virtue, it was a perfect demonstration of what happens when you try to transplant European living unchanged into the bush. It kept reminding me of that blind fireplace in the house in Bafwali. We all sat around the table chewing at the stuff and telling Gérôme how wonderful it was to have a real European meal again, just like being in Brussels.

Gabrielle sat across the table from me. Whatever she might be doing to her napkin while her hands were in her lap, she was her usual calm and self-confident self above table. Her note was in my pocket. I was glad when Miss Finney

began to yawn after dinner and said she would have to turn
in early. She was still staying at Gérôme's, where she had
stayed while André was sick, and Miss Collins was staying at
the Boutegourdes'. It made Miss Finney a sort of hostess, and
the way everybody jumped up and said they had to go home,
Gérôme must have known that everybody was champing at
the bit to get away. But he was graceful about it and showed
us to the door with a few languid regrets that we couldn't stay
longer.

The three Boutegourdes and Miss Collins went their way,
and Henri walked back to the guest house with me. It was a
brick one-room and imitation-bath job, very pleasant. Albert
had left all my things neatly opened up on the table. Henri
stayed for a cigarette and I was afraid he might stay longer, but
finally he stubbed out the end of it and said good night and
went off. I gave him fifteen minutes to get settled at home, and
started out with my map.

There was plenty of moon for following the paths. They
skirted around back of the station buildings and ran past small
areas of bush, dense black and murmurous in the bluish light.
Gabrielle's X was a small clear grassy plot on a sort of promontory. It dropped off suddenly into the darkness in front, and
was backed up by a solid wall of bush. She wasn't there, and I
stood looking out over the vaporous blank that I could tell was
a valley because the broken lines of the grass fires showed up
bright but far away and below me, wavering, flaring, and fading
in their irregular patterns. "Hello."

She had stepped out of the bush behind me, bush that
looked so thick that you'd have thought nothing but a snake
could have pushed through it.

She came up beside me and we stood for a minute looking
at the fires. "The natives set them," she said. "They set them to
drive the game into range, and just let them burn out by themselves. They can't go too far, they always reach the bush, and
you can't burn that."

"How'd you get through that tangle?" I asked.

"There's a path. I didn't think you could follow it so I made you go around on your map. I know all these paths, I could do them blindfolded. This one's awfully pretty in daylight. Let's sit down here."

"It's a nice spot," I said. "I never had a date in one like it before." We sat near the edge of the promontory.

"It's the very end of the station on this side," said Gabrielle. "You follow the path on down and you'd come to the M'buku village." She peered into the space for a moment and then pointed to a spot of light not as far away as the grass fires. "See," she said, "that's their gate fire, it burns all night. It's nice up here in the morning. They all file up the path on the side of the hill, coming up toward you. And in the evening they come back this way. They're not supposed to pass this point unless they're working at the station, and we aren't supposed to go into their area either. When you do, you say to anybody you meet, *Mokala bo n'dolo, bo-sendi.* That means *I enter your land in friendship.* If it's a woman you've met, she'll get down on her knees in the path before you and smile and clap her hands together to show you're welcome."

"That's very pretty," I said. "It doesn't tie in with all that business we were talking about last night."

"The rebellion," she said. "That won't ever happen again. Anyhow they have more gracious little customs among themselves than you'd ever expect. 'Oop, I feel awful."

"What's the matter?"

"Do you really have to go tomorrow?"

"I'd better. I have to catch that plane and I need some leeway."

"You could take a later one. We're just beginning to get acquainted." Even in that light I could tell what a beautiful smile she gave me. "It's our first date," she said. "You know, I might never have another date in my life."

"You come to America," I said. "You'd have plenty."

Her voice changed. "America!" she said. "I hate this place, 'Oop! You can't imagine! It's—I—" she stopped, but you could feel whatever it was she wanted to say still trying to find words for itself. She stirred restlessly and leaned back on one elbow, half lying down, then sat up again and said, "Give me a cigarette."

She had always refused cigarettes before. I lit this one for her and she sat looking straight ahead and took several puffs, blowing the smoke out quickly, not savoring it, and not relaxing at all.

"Talk to me!" she blurted out at last. "This place—" She stopped and ground the cigarette out on the earth.

"Have you been a lot in New York?" she asked, as if it were a matter of life and death.

"Sure," I said, "lots of times. What's the matter, Gabrielle, you act as if you're about to jump out of your skin."

"That's the way I feel," she said. "I wish I could!" She turned toward me and said, "What's going to happen to me?"

I couldn't answer that one. "I've wondered," I said. "What does happen to girls like you?"

"There aren't any other girls like me," she said. "Do you know what's going to happen to me? Nothing! *Nothing!* I can stay here and rot. Papa hasn't any money, not any at all. He had it all in this old Company. Do you Americans really marry girls without any dowry? Who could I marry anyway?"

"You don't have to get married," I dodged. "You could go to Léopoldville and get a job."

"Of course I have to get married," she said. "And a nice Belgian girl can't go anywhere and work. She can't go without her mother. Maybe I could marry a Portuguese in Léopoldville. A Portuguese! No thanks."

"When I first saw you at the funeral I thought you were the most self-possessed girl I'd ever seen," I said. "Now you act as if you're about to fly to pieces."

"I'm always this way inside," she said. "Mama taught me how to stand still, that's all. You can stand still when you have a nice figure like mine and nobody can tell what's going on inside. I do have a nice figure, haven't I?"

"One of the nicest. Look here, Gaby. Calm down and let's talk about this."

"I wanted to talk about America—New York and places," she said. "Would my figure still be nice in New York?"

"It would be nice anywhere. Tell me what you've done with yourself here."

"Do you want the whole story?"

"As much as you feel like telling," I said. "Want another cigarette?"

"No thanks." She paused and worried her forehead with the palm of her hand for a minute. Then, "It wasn't so bad while Jeannette was alive," she said, speaking more slowly now and looking off across the valley again, not at me. "I used to spend a lot of time with her. We used to—"

"Who was this Jeannette?" I asked.

"Why, Henri's wife. Didn't you know that?"

"I didn't even know he was married," I said.

"Well, he was. They came here five years ago. I was only fourteen then. I'd been to Belgium when I was four and when I was nine, when the Company gave Papa his vacations. It was wonderful to have Jeannette come here. She was awfully lonely; she was the only woman on the place besides Mama. Gérôme and his horrid Jacqueline hadn't come yet. I used to go down to Jeannette's all the time. I thought she was beautiful, and I had a crush on Henri too."

"You and Henri—" I began.

She gave a short burst of something like laughter.

"Henri!" she said. But she left it unexplained.

"Jeannette taught me a lot," she went on. "Of course, Mama taught me too. She taught me all my school, except that last year I went to school in Léopoldville. It took all the money Papa had and more that he's still paying back. Jeannette was always getting books and pictures from Belgium. She's the one who taught me about poetry. I know a lot of poetry. *Mignonne, allons voir si la rose—*" She stopped.

"I like that one. Go ahead," I said.

She recited the whole sonnet, and beautifully. Gather ye rosebuds while ye may, it amounts to. To the virgins, to make much of time.

"That's lovely," I said. "Jeannette must have been a nice person." I understood why I had felt the presence of something more than Henri in that house.

"Oh, she was! She was writing a book here, too, for something to do. I used to tell her some of the stories the natives tell their children. I used to hear a lot of them when Mama had native boys taking care of me, and I never forgot them. Jeannette thought they'd make a book. Stories about where the world came from, and where the dead went, and about magic. Always about magic and always full of fear. The natives are afraid of everything."

"What ever happened to the book?" I asked.

"I suppose Henri has it somewhere," she said. "I'd love to have it but I hate to ask him for it. Jeannette's books mean an awful lot to him."

"Would it surprise you to learn there isn't a book in Henri's house?" I asked. "Not even one?"

"That's silly," said Gabrielle. "Jeannette had stacks of them."

"Just try and find them," I said. "When were you in Henri's house last?"

"Months ago. We don't go to one another's houses unless we're asked. It's the closest we can come to having any privacy."

"Well, he hasn't got any books now."

"Then he's put them away somewhere for just himself to see," she insisted. "You ought to ask him to show you this one Jeannette was working on, though. She was doing illustrations for it too. I don't suppose they were much good but they seemed awfully good to me then. When I began to grow up I depended on Jeannette more than ever, and she was still nice to me. I tagged her around everywhere. At first we used to go out in the bush and have long walks, or we would go to the village and the natives would tell us stories and I'd interpret them for Jeannette. She was thin and delicate looking even when she came here and then she began to get thinner and thinner. Finally Miss Finney told her she had tuberculosis and she had to leave here, but she wouldn't do it."

"Why not?" I asked.

"Because she wouldn't leave Henri," said Gabrielle. "She said she was going to die anyway and she wouldn't do it away from him. Henri couldn't go because then he wouldn't have any job, and he didn't have any money. My God!" she cried out, "we're all prisoners here because we haven't got any money! Jeannette finally just had to stay in bed all the time. I couldn't see her often because she was supposed to rest. She didn't have the right things to eat, and—she died, that's all. She's buried back of that awful little shack she had to live in."

"I wonder why Henri didn't tell me about it," I said.

"He won't ever mention her," Gabrielle said. "It changed him an awful lot. When he first came here he was laughing all the time, and working hard. Papa used to say that Henri would make the station amount to something. I don't feel like talking about Henri."

"I want the rest of it. How did it change him?" I asked.

"First he was quiet all the time," she said. "He stuck in that horrid little house for months. Then he started making those collections of birds and orchids and things, and all those old tubes of germs all over the laboratory. Every time he sees a sick native he can't wait to get a test tube at him. And the time he's spent nursing that little antelope! André was always telling him that if he didn't get to work he was going to report him to the company in Brussels. But Henri just laughed because André was always drunk and never did anything either and they both knew Papa would back up Henri if it came to a showdown. So things kept getting worse and worse around here with nobody doing anything except Papa and he can't do it all alone."

She was talking fast and intensely now. "And then Gérôme came down to check things over, and brought that Jacqueline—I *hate* Jacqueline!—and now—they got caught here by the war and all, and—oh, it's all such a mess!" she cried. "I hate being part of it!"

"You at least got to school in Léopoldville last year," I said.

"That didn't amount to anything," she said. "I didn't see anybody but girls. Even the girls who live in Léopoldville and have a dowry and everything can't get married. All the boys are in the war or else they go to South Africa or somewhere." She sighed and put her head back and gave her hair a push, letting the air get in under it. Then she gave something almost like a laugh and said, "Well, this isn't a very good way to be entertaining on your first date. I'll take that cigarette now if I can still have it."

I lit it for her and noticed that her face was calm again in the flare of the match. She blew the match out and then lay back on the grass. She looked pretty there, her hair so soft and her eyes and mouth softened and enlarged in the faint cool light. She took a few long puffs on her cigarette, the smoke catching what light there was so that it looked faintly luminous itself. Gabrielle reached up with her hand and took hold of mine. There was no mistaking the invitation when she pressed it, but I was so taken by surprise that I went on and asked the question that was already half formed and ready to come out.

"You never answered my question about you and Henri," I said.

She kept hold of my hand and answered slowly, almost indifferently, as if she could say the words without listening to them herself, so they wouldn't break into something she didn't want to lose: "Henri won't have anything to do with anything that reminds him of Jeannette, and I guess I do. If I hadn't been their little stray dog, maybe it would be different. That's all." Her tenseness was gone completely, or else she was doing an awfully good job of controlling herself again, because her voice was low and perfectly even, and the steady warm pressure of her hand began to get under the skin of mine.

She lowered our hands onto her cheek for a minute and then let mine go. I lay back and she threw her cigarette away and we moved together, with my arm under her. After the first kiss she took my hand and laid it across her breast. Before long I knew I had to stop, and I tried, but she kept her arms tight over my shoulders. "Don't go away," she murmured.

"I've got to," I said, "I've got to stop now or not at all."

"Don't worry," she said. Her voice was only a whisper, and I could feel her lips moving against my cheek. "Don't worry. It's happened before, lots of times before." And by the time I discovered she had lied to me, it was too late.

Afterward we lay there a long time, smelling the smoke of the grass fires, I remember. I don't know what she was thinking, but I was cursing myself for a damn fool.

I walked a little way off and watched the bright lines of the grass fires creeping and changing pattern. When I came back she had moved a little way down the hill and was half-lying there propped up on her elbow, looking out over the valley. I sat down nearby and said, "It hadn't happened before."

"No."

"Are you all right?"

"Yes, I'm all right."

That seemed to be all there was to say for a while, until she said she wanted another cigarette. She began smoking it slowly, always looking out across the valley instead of at me. "It's late," I said. "You'd better be getting home."

"I guess so." But she didn't move.

I waited, and then finally I said, "You shouldn't have told me that."

"I wanted it to happen."

"There's no use being sorry now," I said.

She turned toward me then and said, "Oh, I'm not sorry! What makes you sorry?"

"You know what makes me sorry," I said.

"That's so silly," said Gabrielle. "I wanted it to happen. I'm sorry if you—was I disappointing?"

"Don't talk like that," I said. I began feeling angry because everything I said sounded prudish.

"Maybe I'd better go home." She held up a hand and I helped her to her feet.

"How are you going to get in without your folks knowing?" I asked. My watch said two in the morning.

"Don't worry," she said. "I'll manage."

We started walking back, Gabrielle going first because she knew the paths. We went into the thick wall of bush and it seemed to open up before her as she went through. She walked along the path without hesitating, making hardly a sound, although as I followed the glimmer of her white dress, things cracked and swished around my feet. When we came to the edge of the bush I could see the laboratory not far off, so I knew where I was.

We stopped just inside the edge, standing close together but not touching, and she said to me, "I'll go alone from here. Don't worry, I can get in." She reached out and took my hand. "I'll see you tomorrow?" she said.

"At Gérôme's, for breakfast," I said. Everybody was coming to see me off.

"Yes. But I mean after that."

"But I'm leaving. You know that."

She recoiled and clutched my hand tighter. "You mean you're going to leave anyhow? After this?"

"I've got to," I said.

"Please stay."

"I've got to go," I said. "I have my plane reservation."

"You've got priorities," she said. "You know you can get on the next one. You can't go!"

"I've got to."

She gave a short suppressed cry and jerked her hand away spasmodically so that I thought for a moment she was going to slap me. But she didn't, and I saw she was crying at last. "Oh, Lord!" I said. I felt rotten and desperate. "Don't, Gabrielle. I can't stay. Even if I could, we couldn't meet like this again."

She got her voice under control.

"Supposing I have a baby," she said.

"Oh, Lord!" I said again. "Oh, sweet, loving, Je—"

"Stop it!" said Gabrielle, and I knew I was acting like an ass.

"I'm sorry," I said.

"You'll stay for a little while, won't you?" she asked.

I said, "No."

Gabrielle was silent for the space of several breaths.

"All right," she said. "If that's how you feel. Good night, 'Oop."

"Good night, Gabrielle. Are you sure you're all right?"

"I'm all right. Good night."

"Good night."

I wanted to say something else or do something else but I couldn't, so I turned away and left her standing there, and walked on back to the guest house and packed and set my alarm clock, and went to bed. I thought I would stay awake, but I didn't. I lay there thinking things over for a little while and then went to sleep.

# CHAPTER FOUR

## Mary Finney

EVERYBODY WAS THERE at breakfast to see me off except Gabrielle and Miss Finney. Madame Boutegourde said Gabrielle had a little headache and had decided to stay in bed. Miss Collins said she had a note for me from Miss Finney, and she presented it to me with a faint cough of apology and backed off giving the impression, somehow, of wringing her hands.

The note said:

H. T.—
Going with you.
Don't leave without me.
Forgot serum.
Yrs. M. F.

"She forgot the serum," coughed Miss Collins gently. "She's got all these natives to inoculate the next two weeks and here she goes and forgets to bring the serum. I never knew

Mary to be so careless before." She looked rather satisfied at
the discovery of this defection on Miss Finney's part, then she
appeared to suffer remorse for her unChristian reaction. "Dear
Mary," she added.

"How's she going to get back?" I asked.

"She'll come back on the *poste*," said Miss Collins.

"There's plenty of serum in Costermansville but if we wait
to send for it by the *poste* that's three days from now, and then
it wouldn't make the return *poste* until next time, and this way
Mary can get it here on the first trip, and anyhow we'll save
gas, and wear and tear on our station wagon, and—oh, for
goodness sake, Mr. Taliaferro, Mary wants a ride with you and
that's that."

Madame Boutegourde had brought a big box of lunch to
take along in the truck, and Henri had brought me the little
black ivory fetish of a figure holding its belly. "Albert raised
hell," he said. "He's sure he's going to die of bellyache if this
thing goes out of the house." Papa Boutegourde was as jovial and
friendly as ever but it seemed to me that Madame Boutegourde
was having to put on, just a little bit, to be pleasant to me. But
when your conscience is hurting you the way mine was, even if
you keep telling yourself that there's no reason for it, you can
imagine all kinds of things. So I put Madame Boutegourde's
coolness down to my imagination. Miss Finney didn't take long
in throwing a few things into a bag, and she showed up in time
for us to get a good start, with her black doctor's bag along too.
Everybody waved us off and I said good-by to the Congo-Ruzi
with feelings so mixed that I didn't know how I felt.

The truck wasn't very comfortable but Miss Finney said
she liked it. She was just right for a traveling companion, just the
opposite of Father Justinien. She enjoyed watching the country
but all she ever said about it was "Nice over there," or something
like that. About ten o'clock she brought out a can of lemon drops
and it was pleasant to suck at them as we rode along.

By eleven o'clock we were both hungry so Miss Finney
decided to break into the lunch box.

"Want to stop, or can you eat while you drive?" Miss Finney asked me.

"I can eat while I drive," I said.

"Good," she said. "Stop a minute anyhow. Pick out a good place. You know."

I drew up by the side of the road where the bush wasn't too thick and Miss Finney climbed out of the truck. She turned back to me and said, "You'd better take advantage of this stop yourself, young man. For crying out loud, you needn't act so funny about it. Anybody can see you haven't been out here very long. You're as bad as Emily." She went crashing off into the bushes.

After we got going again we didn't talk much, just rode along enjoying the ride and Madame Boutegourde's sandwiches. "Nice of Angélique to fix this up for us," said Miss Finney, and then I just about ran the truck into the ditch, because she said, "Think she knows about you and Gaby?" Before I could get an answer together Miss Finney raised a palm at me and said, "Don't ask me what do I mean. You know what I mean. You didn't fall for that serum gag, did you? I don't forget things. I wanted a chance to talk to you, that's all. Listen, Hoop, I haven't got any time to fool around with the delicate approach. I never was any good at it and after half a lifetime of the kind of doctoring I've been doing I don't see any point in it. What the hell, Hoop. I like watching people and figuring them out and trying to figure why they do what they do. Do you think I haven't been watching you and Gabrielle?"

"All right then," I said, "so you've been watching me and Gabrielle."

"I've even been helping you out, God forgive me," she said. "You remember yesterday when Gabrielle gave you the map of the place to meet her? I didn't give a hoot about that culture of Henri's, I just wanted to keep him out of the room. Remember I was in there with Gabrielle when all of you first came in? What do you think I was telling her to do, anyhow, avoid you? And I was going to find some way to get rid of Henri last night too, except that Father Justinien left."

"Any chance of meeting him on the road?" I asked.

"He went the other direction, heaven be praised," said Miss Finney. "Don't try to get me off the track, I'm on it to stay. Remember last night how I said I was so sleepy, right after dinner? Well, I never felt fresher in my life, but I had to go toss around in bed so I could get that party broken up for you and Gaby."

"Well for crying out loud," I said.

Miss Finney laughed. Then she looked more serious than usual and said, "I'm beyond being shocked by what happened, even if I am awfully fond of Gaby. I delivered her, with nobody to help me but Emily, and I've taken care of her, more or less, ever since. I guess I sort of sic'd her onto you. I don't guess there's any chance of getting you to marry her, is there?" All I did was swallow hard, but it was enough of an answer. Miss Finney sighed. "I'm really disappointed," she said. "The way you ogled her in that white dress at the funeral and at dinner that night, I was sure we had the right approach. I guess I'm not much of a matchmaker."

"Matchmaker!" I said. "Miss Finney, if you're talking about what I'm afraid you're talking about, you've got the most brutal direct approach to matchmaking I've ever seen." Miss Finney looked as nearly embarrassed as I ever saw her look.

"I see what you mean," she said. "Maybe I did bring it right down to fundamentals. To tell you the truth, though," she admitted, "I didn't know things would go as far as they did." She looked at me with a sort of exaggerated respect that was about ninety per cent mocking. "You're more of a ripsnortin' young buck than you look," she said. "The academic atmosphere must have changed a lot since I went to college." I concentrated on the road. I could feel my lips pressed tight together and my brows scowling, and I couldn't say anything at all. Miss Finney kept silent for a long few minutes, and I could feel her looking at me as if she were sizing me up. Finally she gave a cross between a laugh and a snort and I glanced over at her. She smiled and shook her head from side to side as if to say, "My, my, my," while she kept looking at me and smiling. I couldn't help it, I felt one side of my mouth going up and finally I had to break down and smile at her too, but I felt like an awful fool.

"Attaboy!" Mary Finney said. "For goodness sake, Hoopie, let's not spar around with each other. I haven't even started to talk, yet. Gaby told me all about it this morning. She wanted me to make sure she was all right and she wanted to know if she was likely to have a baby. I told her no, what with the first time and all. Maybe you'll be lucky, though."

"What do you mean, lucky though?" I said.

"I mean maybe you'll be lucky enough for it to take," Miss Finney said calmly. "If Gabrielle's pregnant I'm going to see that you marry her. Understand? And I'll be doing you a favor. Why don't you marry her anyway?"

"It's not the way I want to get married," I said. "I'm not in love with her."

Miss Finney looked ready to hit me. An indescribable sound came out of her which had probably been uttered many times before, but only by enraged cow elephants. "Love!" she fairly yelled. "Oh, piffle! Piffle, *piffle*, PIFFLE! Honest to God, men are the damnedest fools! The Europeans don't think about anything but dowries and the Americans don't think about anything but a lot of romantic twaddle. Not in love with Gabrielle! My God, what do you think marriage is? You couldn't find a better wife than Gabrielle no matter how far you looked."

"Miss Finney," I said, "there's no use talking about it."

"Why do you go on calling me Miss Finney?" she asked. "You could call me by my first name."

"It wouldn't sound right to me," I said. "Maybe I could call you Miss Mary, though."

"That's the dirtiest, meanest, low-downest remark anybody ever made to me," said Miss Finney, and began to sulk.

Even if Miss Finney had stopped talking, she had got me to worrying about things again. Not about marrying Gabrielle, because I had never had any idea of that, but just about the whole cockeyed situation. In spite of the way Gabrielle had made things happen, I couldn't get over the silly idea that I owed her something and I oughtn't to be going off like this. But there wasn't anything I could do by going back. There wasn't anything I could do at all, except marry her, which I didn't owe her and which I just couldn't see myself doing, romantic twaddle or no romantic twaddle. Damn Miss Finney anyhow, I thought.

"Go ahead," said Miss Finney out of a clear sky, "cuss me."

"Don't think I couldn't," I told her.

"Don't take it so hard," she said. "That's the trouble with people like you and Emily. You get the body and soul all mixed up until you don't know where you're at."

"Stop comparing me to Emily," I said.

"You're a lot like her in a complicated way that's too hard to explain," Miss Finney said. "If you had skirts you'd be pulling at them all the time."

"And also you're a fine one to tell me not to take it so hard," I went on. "I had it all settled in my mind and now you've got it stirred up again. How do you suppose Gabrielle feels?"

"I know how I'd feel in her place," said Miss Finney. "I'd feel disappointed. But if you mean would I feel brokenhearted, no I wouldn't. You're not getting the idea that she's in love with you any more than you're in love with her, are you?"

That was a sock in the teeth, because sure enough I was beginning to have a picture of Gabrielle as a sort of Ariadne back at the Congo-Ruzi.

"Well," said Miss Finney slowly and with great emphasis, "I *will*—be—damned!" I could feel myself getting red. She said, "What makes you think you're so attractive? Of course you're attractive, but only the way any healthy decent looking young man is attractive. You're the best bet that ever came through the Congo-Ruzi station, even so, and I love Gabrielle and I thought it was worth our while to try to get you for her, pickings being as slim as they are in this vicinity."

"Many thanks."

"Not at all," said Miss Finney. "You men make me sick. The way this goddamn world is set up, you're in a bull market, or a bear market or something, whatever it is. Anyhow just by sheer sociological luck you've got something to sell that every woman wants, and all I'm talking about is security."

She was speaking in that way she had, when the words were pretty harsh but somehow the good nature never leaving the way she said them. I had to smile when I turned to her and said, "You seem to know an awful lot about it."

"I'm talking from experience, if that's what you're hinting at," she said. "And I do know how Gabrielle feels, the way you asked. I know exactly how she feels," she said, in a sort of flat voice. "I've just buried the only man I ever tried to get."

"André de l'Andréneau!" I said.

"That's right," she said. "André. I got my fill of the Congo and the prospects of spinsterhood after I'd been out here a few years." It was getting harder for her to talk. "I guess I threw myself at him. I lost my virginity, for whatever that was worth. But André didn't come across for me any more than you're coming across for Gabrielle. I guess that makes me pretty much of a fool for trying the same technique on you and Gaby."

She had dropped her hard, half-bantering manner altogether. There was a silence until finally I managed an "I appreciate your telling me. I thought at the funeral you were the only one who looked at him as if you were really saying good-by."

She looked out over the country half-absently and said, "Emily would die if she ever found out. I don't know why I felt like telling you. I don't even think about it much, most of the time. Some people you tell things to and some you don't." Then she picked up a little more of her old manner and said, "You're not half as good-looking as André was at your age. And of course the worst thing that could have happened to me would have been to catch him. It didn't go on very long, then we had it all out and neither of us ever mentioned it again. But the damn fool always thought he broke my heart."

"Are you sure about that?" I asked.

She saw what I meant. "I'm sure my heart wasn't broken," she said sharply, "or if it was it doesn't make any difference now. Now for God's sake stop talking about it."

"O.K. by me," I said. "You started it."

We rode along for a long time, then, before she burst out, "Once and for all, Hoop, can I talk you into marrying Gabrielle?"

"No," I said.

"You damn fool," she said. That time she really stopped talking, and we just kept on riding. It was the middle of the afternoon before the thing happened that began the end of the adventure.

This woman didn't look as much as thirty-five, not until you hunted for it. She was quite small and trim, with a lot of mascara on her eyelashes, and dark hot-looking reddish hair that had a bleached streak at one temple. She had on linen slacks and a halter that showed her bare pinched-in midriff and a couple of ribs—a little too skinny, but very fashionable somehow even in the heat and the dust, and with an immediately suggestive figure. She was smaller than I remembered, and a little older, and the bleached streak in the hair was new—it was a fad, all the women in Léopoldville were doing it that summer—but the minute I saw her I knew it was the woman I had seen in André de l'Andréneau's room in Bafwali. It was like a tune that you had heard once and couldn't remember, and couldn't reconstruct, but the minute you heard it again you recognized it for sure, and could go on and sing the rest of it.

We were stopping at the lower of the way-stations between Ruzi-Busendi and Costermansville. We needed gas and we needed some beer or lemonade or whatever they would have to drink except the kind of water they would have, and as we drove up, Miss Finney recognized the dusty Dodge standing there.

"Why, it's Jacqueline!" she said. "You know—Gérôme's wife."

We climbed out of the truck, and when we went into the rest-house, Jacqueline de l'Andréneau was sipping a beer at the one table. She turned and jumped up with a cry of recognition when she saw Miss Finney. It was enough like the time she had gasped and wheeled about when I came into the room in Bafwali to suggest the whole thing. Her eyes flickered over me for an instant and then left me so quickly that I knew she had recognized me too.

She was all over Miss Finney then, calling her *ma chère* and so on, in a very affected and very beautiful *Comédie-Française* French, studied to the last little syllable until it came out fast and throaty and without hesitation.

"This is Hoopie Taliaferro," said Miss Finney, jerking her head my way. "You missed him."

"*Enchantée*," she *Comédie-Française*d me. Then she added that she was desolated to have missed me at the Congo-Ruzi. She held out a soft, thin hand, tiny, with lacquered nails, and when I pressed it I could feel the bones move. I kept it a moment overtime. Her eyes flickered again, on and off my face. She had the kind of good looks so many French women have—the nose too large and bony for real beauty, but an alive quality to the face that attracted you right away, and a frank use of every artifice of make-up to enhance whatever good points her features had. Jacqueline de l'Andréneau concentrated everything on making you notice her eyes, which were very dark with clear whites, and sparkled as she flickered them about. Her mouth was the brightest most artificial red.

She pulled at her hand and I let it go, but I said, "Haven't we met before?"

"Of course not," she said. She always spoke so artificially that she could make an easy lie. "I am in Léopoldville while you are here. Your Mr. Slattery told me about you."

"He told me about you, too," I said.

She hid her suspicion almost immediately.

"How sweet of him," she said.

Miss Finney said, "Oh, goo, goo, goo. You two haven't got the time to get anywhere with each other, you might as well lay off it."

"Funny," I said to Jacqueline. "I could have sworn I saw you in Bafwali."

"Of course not," said Jacqueline again, more sharply. She turned to Miss Finney and they went into a lot of talk about where Miss Finney was going, and when she would be back. The talk was mostly Jacqueline's, all throaty and full of exclamations. Miss Finney just grunted out her answers. And then she said, "Too bad you missed the funeral."

"Oh, my dear!" said Jacqueline. "Then it is all over? Poor André!" She took one of Miss Finney's hands in both of hers; they looked like fancy decorations on a well-baked ham. "And Gérôme—how is Gérôme?"

"Oh, Gérôme's O.K.," said Miss Finney. "How're you?" She didn't even pretend to hide her dislike, but Jacqueline pretended not to notice it.

"But exhausted!" she said. Her voice became appropriately fainter and lower. "Such a shock, so unexpected, and this dreadful trip back. My dear, I—"

"Well," interrupted Miss Finney, "we'd better be getting on. Tell the lady good-by, Hoopie. Jacqueline, you be sure to give Henri my love when you see him."

Jacqueline didn't quite spit in Miss Finney's eye.

"Good-by, Mr. Taliaferro," she said, turning to me and baring her teeth. "I can't tell you how sorry I am to have missed your visit."

"Perhaps another time," I said.

"How nice that would be," said Jacqueline, as one would say, "May you boil in oil."

They had our tank filled by then so we went on out and drove off, everybody waving to everybody else.

"You forgot you wanted something to drink," I said to Miss Finney.

She said, "I can't take in food or drink when I'm around that—that—"

"Bitch?" I suggested.

"You know everything, don't you," said Miss Finney.

"What was going on in there?" Miss Finney asked me after we got started again. "First I thought you two were trying to make each other, and then I was afraid I wouldn't get you out of there before she bit your jugular in two."

"I know something about Jacqueline," I said. I decided to tell it. There was too high a potential in the whole business to pass it up any longer, respect for the dead or no respect for the dead. "I really did see her in Bafwali."

Miss Finney jerked around and looked at me with wild speculation.

"If you're going to say what I think you're going to say—where in Bafwali? Oh, Mary Finney, you dummy! Hoop, I feel a tie-up. Oh, Lord, there's something here!" She was acting like a kid about to be let in on a secret, but then the brightness drained out of her face and something between puzzlement and anxiety came into it. "I don't know," she said, "it might be bad, this tie-up. Go ahead."

"I just saw her for a minute but I'm sure it was Jacqueline," I said. "In the de l'Andréneaus' house in Bafwali. André didn't know she was there. Of course I didn't know who André was, at the time. And he didn't know who I was, yet. Then he left and I didn't know Jacqueline was in the bedroom—"

"My God," said Miss Finney, "didn't anybody know anything? Start over again, Hoop, and slow it down."

I went over the whole thing for her. From time to time she looked as if she might explode if she didn't say something, but she would always just say "Go on!" She was so intent that her lips parted and I could hear the breath going through them. A little more and I could have heard her brain clicking, too.

When I finished, she turned around straight again and pulled off her helmet and rested her head against the back of the seat. She closed her eyes and took a deep breath as if she were settling down to go to sleep. "Don't say anything to me for a while, Hoop," she said.

You'd have thought she was asleep except that the hard, blunt nail of one finger kept tapping the helmet in her lap. And from time to time she would breathe out a half-formed exclamation.

She opened her eyes once and said, "What was the exact date?"

"July first," I said. "I've been counting back, and it was July first."

"Why'd you count back?"

"Because I got a letter from my boss in Léopoldville saying she was in town for our Fourth of July party."

Miss Finney beat her brow. "Mary Finney, you fleabrain!" she said. "Of course it works out. Of course she spent an afternoon and night in Bafwali between planes. Then another day to get to Léopoldville. Then give her the third for sharpening her claws and putting on her war paint. If your boss had fireworks on the fourth, I bet they weren't a patch on Jacqueline. All right, I'm thinking again. Don't drive too fast, Hoop, we may be turning around and going back."

"Boloney," I said.

But she closed her eyes again, and it must have been fifteen minutes before she opened them and sat up with the air of having settled everything. She looked alert and quick, but not tense.

"All right, Hoop," she said. "Go back."

"Nothing doing," I said.

"Goddamnit, turn this truck around and go back," she said, in a voice like a bear-trap closing.

"You're the boss from now on if it's that important," I said, and stopped the truck.

"It's that important and you're damn right I'm the boss," Miss Finney said. She turned to me and said penitently, "I'll try to stop swearing, Hoop. I do need your help."

"You've got it," I said.

It had been an hour since we left Jacqueline at the waystation. She had better than a two hours' start on us in a car that could go faster than our truck.

I drove along waiting for Miss Finney to begin talking, because I knew she wouldn't until she was ready. Pretty soon she began.

❄ ❄ ❄

"Dysentery," said Miss Finney, "is a disease as old as man. It is referred to in some of the most ancient writings on medicine. Naturally I've seen dysentery cases by the thousands, but I never saw one like André's before. That's why I was so fussy about having those slides and cultures. You diagnose this stuff from clinical manifestations and half the time you make a mistake. But when the laboratory says it's amoebic, it's amoebic."

"What made you so fussy?" I asked. "Didn't you trust Henri?"

"I don't trust anybody, not any more than I can help," she said. And then she gave me that long speech I've already put in, the one about white men's false faces in the tropics, and about how she always looked twice at people, once on the surface and then a good long time underneath, trying to find out what they're really like. "I don't mean this to be a lecture on Henri," she finished. "I mean it about everybody. I wasn't afraid Henri had any reason to fool me, but he might be careless. Well, it was amoebic all right—no room for doubt. I collected the dejecta myself and kept check while we searched for the amoebae. We did that on a slide, of course. The culture was a sort of side experiment. I wanted it to compare with Henri's other dysentery cultures. The thing that worried me about André was that I never had seen amoebic come on so fast or work so quick. You can carry that stuff around with you as long as thirty years and never die from it or even have anything worse than recurrent inconvenience. Or I've seen it take them off after a few weeks. Acute onset's always the gravest form, I already knew that, but André's case was at the extreme limit as far as speedy development was concerned. He must have swallowed enough bugs to infect a regiment. And I don't understand how that could have happened in the normal run."

"What's so suspicious about it?" I asked. "It could happen to anybody, couldn't it?"

"It *could*," Miss Finney admitted, "but here André had been out in this country going on thirty years, and he never picked it up. Some people seem to have a greater susceptibility to it than others. And then André wasn't a fool, anyway, not when it came to routine precautions against disease. They get to be second nature. Anyhow he was one of the toughest specimens I ever saw. The way he abused his body with liquor and everything else, he ought to have killed himself long ago, but he never even got sick. Then all of a sudden he comes down with this stuff and out he goes, in a matter of days. Sure, it could happen to anyone, and if he'd had a mild case I'd have taken it for granted. But a thing like this! Remember that time in Chicago during the World's Fair?—1933, I think, when they had an outbreak of the stuff. That night club woman, Texas Somebody, she died of it along with a lot of others. Well, those were supposed to be especially violent primary infections. The people began to develop symptoms eight or ten days after infection and they went out pretty quick. But André was already having belly cramps when he showed up at the station on the fifth of July, and that means it only took four days to develop."

I felt cold and thin for a minute. "What are you trying to say?" I asked her. "You're counting back to something that happened in the house in Bafwali."

"I only mean that André's infection wasn't a normal one. It would be hard to get infected as badly as he was without trying. Or without somebody doing it for you—feeding you more bugs than you'd ever pick up by any accident I can imagine. I'm not figuring on anything but arithmetic and geography. Arithmetic says that since a case as severe as this one should have started showing symptoms four or five days after infection, infection occurred about July first. Geography says that André and Jacqueline were together that day, and anybody could tell Jacqueline was ready to rip you to pieces because you knew she'd been there. Ordinarily Jacqueline likes her young men whole. I guess I'm figuring on something besides arithmetic and geography after all. I hate Jacqueline. She's rotten mean. She's spoiled and she's desperate and she's got the conscience of a storm-trooper. The only thing I can't figure out is what she could get out of feeding André a culture of amoebae. She's in the same spot now that she was before he died, so far as I can see—or worse, because now Gérôme would have to stay out here to manage things even if they had the money to get away."

I asked, "If she had a culture of this stuff she had to get it somewhere. Are you still trying to drag Henri into this?"

"I said I wasn't, and I'm not," said Miss Finney. "Not any more than I'm trying to drag Gérôme or the Boutegourdes or Emily, or Father Justinien and Albert for that matter." She considered for a moment and then said reflectively, "Henri. Maybe that's worth working on. But anybody could go in the laboratory and pick up some of that stuff. Henri always had cultures of everything lying all around, just the way he does everything. Everybody's in and out of there, from Gabrielle on up. They never lock the buildings."

"I suppose you know what you're saying," I said. "You're accusing Jacqueline of murder."

"Not quite," said Miss Finney. She quoted: *"Poison is a woman's weapon.* It would certainly be Jacqueline's. But all I've done so far, Hoop, is put two and two together. I already knew the answer to that one, though—four. Four isn't enough, and so far that's all the figures I've got, just two and two. I'll damn well accuse Jacqueline of murder if I get enough figures to add up to the total I'm after, you can depend on that."

She got all the rest of the figures during the next twenty-four hours. She got a lot of them from me, without my knowing what they meant. Because now she asked me to do the talking, and to tell her everything I could remember that I had said and done with everybody at the Congo-Ruzi. I talked almost all the way back to Ruzi-Busendi, until my voice was so tired that it came out all weak and fuzzy. But she wanted to know every little thing, because she said I wouldn't have any idea what was important or what wasn't. Now and then she would nod her head and say, "That fits in," or "That's out of key," or she would ask me to go over some incident again thinking hard, to try to get all of it. I told her everything I could remember, very much as I have written it down here, so far.

# CHAPTER FIVE

## Dodo

THERE WERE NO LANTERNS for us at Ruzi-Busendi this time. The little shack where Madame Boutegourde had waited for Father Justinien was swallowed up in the black silhouette of the encroaching bush, and I'd have gone past it if Miss Finney hadn't checked me. We had made poor time getting back. The truck had begun to sputter and cut out, and I had had to stop and blow out a feed line. It cost me a nasty mouthful of gasoline, and the truck ran well for only half an hour until it began to overheat. This time it was the fan belt, flapping around in shreds. There was a spare in the tool box and I managed to get it on, but what with one thing and another we didn't get in to Ruzi-Busendi until close to midnight. It was a good half hour after that up the bumpy road to Henri's, which was the first house you came to.

With the ailing truck and with all the talking I had done for Miss Finney, and with the gasoline taste making me feel sick at my stomach, I felt more than all in. I was jumpy and nervous, and for all I tried to hold the wheel steady, the truck would careen every time an animal ran across the road. A night bird flew into our headlights and made a thud that brought with it a picture of sticky feathers plastered against the radiator. I don't like the word "nervous" but that's what I was, tired and nervous, with the feeling that everything was wrong and against me, the way you get when you're tired out but have to keep going. When we reached Henri's lane I turned into it automatically, just because I had done it the first night I drove up that road. I wasn't planning to stay with Henri. He would be asleep, and anyway Miss Finney said the guest house wouldn't be locked. As for her, she would just have to try to get into the Boutegourdes' without waking anybody, and crawl in with Emily. She wasn't going to stay at Gérôme's any more, not with Jacqueline in the same house.

"Then why don't I stay at Henri's after all and give you the guest house?" I said. We were stopped in the lane, with the headlights pointed toward Henri's, but there were no lights burning tonight and our headlights showed us only the sharp brilliance of the bush nearby and the dense black beyond it. The faintly luminous sky overhead was all but blotted out by the overhanging bush on either side of the lane. There was nobody to overhear us, but in that oppressive tunnel of foliage you felt impelled to speak low. Miss Finney almost whispered to me, her voice just more than audible above the continuous murmuring of the bush around us. "No," she began, "take me to the Boutegourdes'—" but she never finished it because two shots crashed close together through the air ahead of us. It was so sudden that I felt that the bush had been blasted away, leaving us exposed before some malevolent adversary. Then the stillness flowed back around us like the sea filling a great hole, and everything was exactly as it had been before.

We sat there stupefied until Miss Finney snapped into life and said, "It's at Henri's. Get us down there." I threw the truck into gear, and when I try to remember it just the way it happened I can't get any impression except that we were lifted up and set down, in the space of a breath, by the little garden in front of Henri's house. But I remember the hoarse screaming—scream, silence, scream, silence—that stopped just as we got there.

There was a flashlight lying on the grass in front of the house, and in its glow we could make out Henri, crouched over close to the ground. I thought he was shot in the belly and bending over to clutch at himself. I was so excited that I didn't have the sense to turn the headlights in Henri's direction, but jumped out of the truck and left them blazing into the veranda.

Miss Finney got there as soon as I did. She must have picked up that flashlight the way a rodeo cowboy picks a handkerchief off the ground at a gallop, because she had it trained on Henri right away. He turned a bewildered face into the light, as if he were wondering where he was and what had happened. He was sitting on his heels, holding the body of the mouse antelope on the palms of both hands, the way you might hold a serving tray. The delicate legs stuck out awkwardly, one of them still quivering, and the head hung down almost severed by the gash across the throat. The blood was flowing out in feeble pulses, drenching Henri's wrists and running down onto his knees.

"It's Dodo!" I cried, and it wasn't relief I felt, but the shock of personal loss, as if it had been a real person murdered there instead of a little animal I had grown fond of.

"Put her down, Henri," said Miss Finney firmly. "You're getting all bloody. Who fired those shots?"

"I did," said Henri. He let Dodo's body slide off his hands onto the grass. "Where's my rifle?"

Miss Finney played the flashlight around the ground and it picked out the rifle lying a few feet back of Henri. "Give him a hand, Hoop," Miss Finney said. "Come on, Henri, you've got to get cleaned up." She breathed out a trembling sigh and I began to feel the same weakness, that watery-kneed feeling that comes with relief from sudden fear.

Henri said, with more color in his voice, "I'd better wash up out here," and we followed him around the house into the back yard where I had seen Albert hanging out the clothes that first day. There were some oil drums full of water lined up by Albert's laundry table and Henri plunged his hands into one of them. He stood there as if he were still a little dazed. He looked down and saw blood on the front of his shirt. He jerked his hands up out of the water and instead of unbuttoning the shirt he wrenched it open with both hands and tore it off and flung it away.

"My God!" he said, coming to life with a rush, his voice rising. "I'm all over blood!" He began ripping his clothes off and in a moment he was naked, splashing water over himself frantically and rubbing his body wherever the blood had soaked through onto it.

"Take care of him, Hoop," said Miss Finney. "I'll be right back." The light of her torch began bobbing across the grass and she went up the back steps onto the veranda and into the house.

"Take it easy, Henri," I said. "You're all right, you've got it all off."

He straightened up and took a deep breath. Then he laughed, still with a quaver in his voice, and began stripping the water from his arms and legs with the palms of his hands. "I don't know what's the matter with me," he said.

"Where's Miss Finney?"

Miss Finney reappeared carrying something big and white hanging over her arm. She came across to us and ran the light up and down over Henri a couple of times.

"You've got a beautiful build," she commented. "Here— take this." The white thing was a sheet. "Dry yourself off before you catch your death of cold. I couldn't find a towel." Henri wrapped the sheet around himself and the two of us rubbed him dry.

"Come on in the house, you," said Miss Finney. "I'm going to put you to bed."

"I guess I've made a fool of myself," Henri said. We started up to the house. "I acted like an old woman, but I'm all right now. I don't have to go to bed."

"You've had a shock of some kind and a dousing in cold water," Miss Finney said. "The doctor says you go to bed. Anyhow I want to hear what happened."

We all went into Henri's bedroom, and Henri sat on the bed with the wet sheet clinging to him, shivering.

"Take that wet thing off and get under the blanket," Miss Finney directed him. He dropped the sheet without the embarrassment I would have felt, and climbed in between the blanket and the remaining sheet.

"You ought to take a lesson from Henri," Miss Finney said, "you and Emily."

"This makes me feel pretty silly," Henri said, "but I was asleep, and it was all of a sudden." He sighed and relaxed against the pillow. You could see that the bed felt good to him, no matter what he said about feeling silly.

I sat on the bed by Henri, and Miss Finney pulled up the only chair. She said, "Now let's try to remember that Dodo is only an antelope after all, and let's get the straight of this. What happened?"

"What time is it?" Henri asked.

Miss Finney looked at her wrist watch. "Going on one o'clock," she said.

"Then I must have been asleep about four hours," Henri said. "I was tired tonight, hadn't been feeling well all day. Stomachache. I hadn't got ready for bed. I thought I would lie down for a minute and I fell asleep." He frowned. "I woke up and I knew there was somebody out there. I suppose the eagle woke me." That was the first time I knew what the screams had been— for that matter it was the first time I was conscious of having heard them. Henri went on, "The flashlight was here by the bed and I got the rifle out of my closet as quickly as I could. I went to the door and I could barely see this figure moving out there, moving away from Dodo's stockade toward the bush. I think I knew right away what it was. Anyway I stood just inside the door and flashed the light on him. All I could tell was that it was a native. He dropped Dodo and began to run for it. The way she fell I knew he had killed her. I fired at him—no, I ran out there before I fired, I don't know why. Anyway I was out there when I fired. If I hadn't had to drop the light to fire, I'd have got him."

"It's a good thing you didn't," said Miss Finney. "You'd have had worse than antelope blood on your hands."

"I suppose so," Henri said.

He had raised himself up on his elbow while he was telling all this, but now he sank back on the pillow again. His face grew white and sweat broke out on it.

"I'm sorry," he said, "but I'm going to be sick," and he leaned over the other side of the bed, and was.

Miss Finney said, "Hoop, run out to the truck and bring me my bag, the black one."

When I got back with the bag, Miss Finney was standing by the bed sopping one corner of the sheet with water from the carafe. She began to bathe Henri's forehead and face with it. "Open the bag for me, Hoopie," she said. I set the bag on the table, and as I begun to undo the catch I noticed a smear of blood on my own hand. I grabbed out my handkerchief and wiped at it. Most of it came off, but it was dried around the edge and stuck to me. "Here," said Miss Finney. She never missed anything. She handed me the sheet and I scrubbed off the dried blood with the wet corner. I put the handkerchief back in my pocket.

Miss Finney came over and opened the bag herself, and took out a syringe and a phial. "You're going to get a hypodermic, my bucko," she said to Henri, and began sucking the stuff up into the syringe.

Henri protested, and said again she was making him feel like a fool, but she gave him the shot. She put the syringe away and closed up her bag. "I never heard of such a ruckus over nothing," she said. "If you two he-men are all right, I'm going to get a little rest. I'll stay here, Hoop. Henri'll be asleep in no time but I'd better stick around."

I cleaned up the mess by the bed so Miss Finney wouldn't have to, and it took another few minutes to help her find sheets for the couch in the living room. When I went in to say good night to Henri he opened his eyes slowly and mumbled something like "—damn nuisance of myself," and closed his eyes again. He was pale and his eyelids twitched. Miss Finney followed me out to the truck. After I had got in and started the motor, she stayed by the side of the truck and I could tell she had something to say.

She said in a voice more troubled and hesitant than I had ever heard her use, speaking very low against the sound of the motor, "Hoop, does something strike you as awfully—what was that word you used this afternoon? Screwy? Does something strike you as being awfully screwy about this whole business?"

"Well, I don't often wind up my day like this," I said.

She brushed this aside with a gesture of irritation.

"I'm serious," she said. "There are half a dozen things about it that worry me. Henri took it too hard, for one thing."

"Dodo was a pet," I said. "I loved her myself."

"Sure, but Henri's no softie," said Miss Finney. "I don't mean you are, Hoop. But if you really knew Henri you'd know what a hard shell he has. He wasn't all wrought up like that just because Dodo was dead. It meant something special to him, something more than the death of a pet."

"It must have been pretty scary, though," I said. "Waked in the middle of the night like that, then the prowler, the sudden excitement, and all that blood."

"That's another thing," said Miss Finney. "Why should anyone kill Dodo just that way?"

"To eat her," I said. "Henri told me that someday some native or some animal would come out of the bush and get her. I thought they were supposed to stay in their own area at night."

"Of course they are," said Miss Finney, "but they don't. They prowl around pretty much at will. I just can't see why he cut Dodo's throat."

"I guess I'm dumb," I said. "I'd say he cut her throat to kill her."

Miss Finney shook her head. "I've seen them break the necks of those little animals with one blow of their hand," she said. "But for that matter, why did he kill her at all? Here he was on the prowl, and he took time to kill her when he could have simply carried her off. You know how Dodo was—she'd let anybody pick her up. And they can't make any noise, those little antelopes, not even a squeak. He didn't need to kill her at all, he didn't need to take the time to. But even if he *had* needed to, why take the extra time and make all that mess? Why all this butchery? See what I mean?"

"You make sense," I said, and I began to have an uneasy feeling, because the more sense Miss Finney made, the less sense Dodo's murder made.

"And that isn't all," sighed Miss Finney. "A lot of other things keep nagging me—won't fit in. I wish the hell I knew what was going on."

"Maybe you've gathered some more figures," I suggested.

"I sure could use an answer book," she grinned. "Well, good night Hoop. Thanks for being a sport."

"Boloney," I said. "See you in the morning."

To reach the guest house you had to go around the loop the road made going through the grounds. You had to pass within sight of Gérôme's house, and the Boutegourdes' too. Gérôme's house was spilling light all over the place. But it had a funny empty look and I slowed the truck to see better. The front door was wide open, which wasn't too unusual since it might have been open in any case, to get the air. But the front screen was hanging open too, and that was where the empty look came from. This was strictly out of line, partly because it would have been latched as a token precaution, but mostly because everything was always closed against the mosquitoes.

I thought of stopping, then I rationalized that it was none of my business. When I came to the Boutegourdes', though, and saw all the lights on there too, I realized that I had been clutching the wheel, expecting to see the lights, and fearing that I would.

There was so much commotion going on inside that I drove the truck up to the front and stopped and got out and went up the steps to the door without anybody paying me any mind. Papa and Madame Boutegourde were bending over the sofa, both of them in bathrobes and Madame Boutegourde with her hair hanging in a tail down her back. There was a third figure too, a small figure in a pale silk robe splashed all over with gigantic red poppies. It took me a minute to realize that this could really be Miss Collins, caught out of her bedroom in this revelation of an inner yearning. She was making mewling sounds, and the Boutegourdes were exclaiming in frightened disconnected phrases of French, but most of the commotion was coming from the couch. Jacqueline was stretched out on it, in a fine fit of hysterics.

She was horrible to hear. She would get herself under control and begin talking in a strange thickened voice, then the idiot laughing or sobbing would break through and she would be off again. She was a different Jacqueline from the one I had seen that afternoon. There were remains of makeup smeared over her face, and her hair was sticking out in every direction. She had on something that looked like red crêpe lounging pajamas; they were ripped and snagged all over, and spotted with dust and stains of moisture. It was a big sofa she was lying on, and she looked smaller and more slippery-boned than ever, writhing like an eel and twitching, and clutching at Papa Boutegourde's bathrobe while she screamed with laughter or choked with sobs.

"You'll have to hit her to get her out of that," I said.

Jacqueline sat straight up on the couch and when she saw me come in the door her eyes popped out like golf balls. "*Rape!*" she screeched, and fell flat on her back again and went into peal after peal of laughter, twisting her fingers together until you would think they would never straighten out again.

"They hurt me!" she whimpered. She began screaming again: "*Oh, Gérôme, my poor Gérôme! Where's Gérôme?* What did they do to you, Gérôme? Oh, Géro-o-o-ôme!" and her voice went off into a long howl. Then she collapsed and lay there heaving, with hiccoughs jerking out of her.

"*Brandy!*" yelled Madame Boutegourde into thin air, and Papa hurried away. "My God, Monsieur Taliaferro, what are you doing here?"

"I came back," I said inanely. "What's the matter?"

Miss Collins said, "Jacqueline doesn't feel well."

Jacqueline moaned.

"Oh, my God," said Madame Boutegourde. It was "*Ah, mon Dieu!*" and was more a prayer than profanity. "What can we do? She came here like this, running, she fell right into the room—only a few minutes ago. She says Gérôme—oh, I don't know what. She can't talk straight. *César!*" she called. Papa came running with a glass of brandy. He knelt down and supported Jacqueline with one of his thick little arms, lifting up her shoulders. The way she folded together under the uplifting pressure made me think of the way the bones in her hand had moved when I took it that afternoon. Papa Boutegourde pressed the glass of brandy against her lips, but she moaned and made bubbly and snuffly noises into the glass so that the brandy spilled over.

Miss Collins said, "If she won't drink it, throw it on her."

Jacqueline whimpered and downed the brandy in a couple of gulps.

"You've got to find Gérôme," she said, fairly normally, but still in that strange thick voice. It gave me the feeling you get when the dentist stuffs the little wads of gauze under your lip while he's working on you. Jacqueline was quiet enough now so that I could see that her mouth didn't look funny only because the lipstick was smeared. It was bruised and swollen on one side, and the bluish flush spread on up into her cheek.

"*Regardez-ça!*" cried Madame Boutegourde suddenly. "Look at that!" She had lifted one of Jacqueline's hands to chafe the wrist, and the loose sleeve of the pajama coat slid back to the elbow. Her wrist was bruised. You could see the finger marks, and when Madame Boutegourde pushed the sleeve on up to the shoulder, there they were again, on the upper arm.

"My God!" said Madame Boutegourde again, "she's not pretending!" She caught her breath then because she had admitted what I suppose we had all been half-feeling. Jacqueline had never done or said one single natural thing in the presence of anybody in that room, and in spite of the way she looked it wasn't until we began to see that somebody had really been giving her a going-over that we began to take her seriously.

"They hurt me," Jacqueline moaned, and even then I couldn't help suspecting some theatrical self-pity. "Gérôme! Oh, please, they've got him, go find him, César!" Now she lay back on the pillow and began crying in a helpless, despairing kind of way that would have been heartrending in anybody else. "You all hate me," she said, "and you won't help me. Oh, Gérôme, Gérôme!"

"What are you talking about?" said Papa Boutegourde roughly. "Pull yourself together and tell us what happened, if you want help. What happened to Gérôme?"

"I don't know," sobbed Jacqueline. "They took him away."

Miss Collins said, "Mr. Taliaferro, where's Mary? We've got to get Jacqueline fixed up so she can talk."

"She's down at Henri's," I said.

"Took him away where?" Papa Boutegourde was prodding Jacqueline.

I thought of something. "Where's Gabrielle?" I asked.

Madame Boutegourde said, "Asleep, thank God."

"She can't be," I said. I felt as if a piece of ice had been clamped against the nape of my neck. "Not in all this racket." Madame Boutegourde gave me a wild look and went out of the room.

"Go get Mary," Miss Collins told me. "She'll give Jacqueline something."

Madame Boutegourde's shriek came from the other end of the house. She appeared in the doorway looking like the last acts of all the Greek tragedies rolled into one. "She's gone!" she screamed. "She's not there! Her bed—her window—" She fell into a chair and began giving a good imitation of what Jacqueline had just been doing.

I grabbed Miss Collins by the hand.

"Monsieur Boutegourde," I said, "I know where Gabrielle is. I'll go get her. I'll send Miss Collins back with Miss Finney." Papa Boutegourde was standing frozen in the middle of the room between the two hysterical women. I yanked Miss Collins out the door with me and I have the impression that I flung her into the truck. I tore down the road toward Henri's, glad I had the wheel to hang onto. Miss Collins was bouncing around like a dried pea in a cement mixer. Hell had certainly broken loose at the Congo-Ruzi, and if there was a devil in the bush, the way Miss Finney said, he was out settling scores that night.

Miss Finney was lying on her back with her eyes wide open and her hands under her head. She had a lamp lit on the table, and you'd have thought she didn't have a care in the world. She looked as calm as if she was just lying down for a few minutes' rest after sweeping up the room or something, except that her arms were bare and she had a sheet pulled up under her chin. She made quite a large white hillocky mass under the linen, terminating in a sharp bisected peak that was her toes, sticking straight up.

Miss Collins and I came bursting in and Miss Finney said, "Well, well, it's the Poppy Girl. What's the hurry?"

"There's plenty of hurry, Mary Finney," Miss Collins chattered. "You needn't be lying there that way. Somebody's been beating Jacqueline."

"Lucky him," said Miss Finney, but a change came over her in spite of herself. She continued to lie there. "Don't bother me," she said, "I'm thinking."

Miss Collins stamped her foot. "Get up out of there, Mary," she said. "Jacqueline and Angélique are both about to go crazy. Gabrielle's disappeared, too."

Miss Finney sat up suddenly, clutching the sheet around her.

"Turn your back, Hoop," she said. "I've got on my slip, but I'm not as pretty as Henri. Turn your back and start talking." I turned my back and heard her moving around in a hurry, getting into her clothes. I said, "Everybody's at the Boutegourdes'. Jacqueline's been knocked around by somebody and she says whoever it was took Gérôme away. Gabrielle's gone from her room, slipped out the window, and if you'll get organized here I'll go find her."

Miss Finney said, "Where?"

"I think I know," I said.

"Me too," said Miss Finney. I heard her grunt slightly, probably pulling on a shoe. "Get the hell out of here, Hoop. We'll take Henri's car to the Boutegourdes'."

"Henri all right?" I asked.

"Like a babe," said Miss Finney. "Take this." I felt the flashlight pressed into my hand. "Get out."

As I left the room I heard her saying to Miss Collins, "You look like Sadie Thompson in that getup, Emily." When I got to the laboratory I ran the truck across the open ground to the clump of bush where Gabrielle and I had stopped that night and she had asked me not to leave the Congo-Ruzi. I parked the truck where I thought the path came out, and with the flashlight I found it in a few minutes. I was certain I could follow it, and sure enough it was easy. I could hardly have got off it, anyhow, the bush was so thick on each side of it, but I would have fallen around and spent all night feeling my way, if Miss Finney hadn't been smarter than I was, and sent me off with the light.

I never doubted for a minute that Gabrielle would be out there on the promontory overlooking the valley. She wasn't home, she wasn't at Henri's, and I took it for granted she wasn't at Gérôme's, but I didn't stop to figure things out, or why she wouldn't be at the guest house or the laboratory. She had slipped out, the way she had slipped out to see me. I didn't stop to reason anything, but I suppose I thought all these things in the back of my head. And I was right. I hadn't gone far before I found her cowering there, as far off the path as she could press herself into the tangled growth. My light picked her out, half crouching and pressing herself backwards, her eyes wide and her lips drawing back from her teeth. She was so still that she looked like one of those night photographs of wild animals, where the animals trip off their own flash.

Her voice came out in a croak. "Don't touch me," she said. "Don't touch me." She kept saying it.

"It's Hoop, Gabrielle," I said. She didn't move or change expression. I turned the light up into my own face, so she could see.

I heard her cry come out like something giving way under pressure. Before I got the light back onto her she had flung herself on me, both hands clutching the front of my shirt. I put both arms around her to keep her from falling, and she let go of my shirt and flung her arms around me too. We stood there pressed close together and I could feel the current of her fear, like an actual emanation from her body. She tried to talk but I couldn't get the words, then she began to relax and tremble, and finally she stopped trembling and let her head drop against me and began to cry. I could feel her going limp and I knew she was all right now.

She told me what I could hardly believe, that he was there; then she led me along the path until we came to the clearing where we had been the night before. Gérôme lay there across the path where the promontory dipped down into the valley toward the native village. I remember how he looked in the beam of the flashlight. I could see the gash in his throat and I saw his shirt ripped half off his back and his back dark with blood, but it wasn't until I had taken Gabrielle home and Miss Finney had come back and examined him that we saw how the strip of flesh had been peeled off his shoulder. When Papa Boutegourde and I moved him that night we found the circumcision knife lying there. Moving him was a tough job, but not as tough as I had expected, once we got him on Miss Finney's stretcher and covered him up. We put him in the laboratory and locked it. It was getting light when the three of us, Miss Finney and Papa Boutegourde and I, got back to the Boutegourdes'. Little Emily Collins was sitting straight as a poker in the middle of the living room, with Papa Boutegourde's rifle in her hands.

"They're all quiet," she said. Miss Finney had half the station under hypodermics that night—first Henri, then Jacqueline and Madame Boutegourde, and then Gabrielle.

Miss Collins went on, "I can look after this hospital, Mary. You and Mr. Taliaferro had better lie down, you haven't been to bed at all. You look sick, Mr. Boutegourde."

Papa Boutegourde said, in a voice that came dragging out of him, "You must lie down too, Miss Collins."

Miss Collins said, "Nobody's going to get me out of this chair. I went to bed at eight and I slept five hours."

"You're a brick, Emily," said Miss Finney. "I'll go down to Henri's. I'm not easy about him."

I told Miss Finney she shouldn't stay at Henri's alone. She pooh-poohed the idea but finally she gave in, and we left Miss Collins sitting there guarding everybody else while we went on down to Henri's. Henri was sprawled all over the bed like something hit by a freight train. I found enough cushions to make a pallet on the floor near by. I lay down, and heard the couch in the next room creak as Miss Finney lowered herself onto it.

"You all right?" I called.

"Don't bother me, Hoopie," she said. "I'm thinking." I imagined her lying there on her back, her hands behind her head, her toes pointing up. Then I went to sleep, or passed out, whichever you want to call it, until she came in and shook my shoulder. The sunlight was brilliant. Miss Finney had made coffee.

Of the three of us, Miss Finney looked the freshest.

When Henri and I went out to throw a couple of buckets of water over each other in the back yard, we saw that his clothes of the night before had been picked up and hung on the bushes nearby. Miss Finney had taken care of Dodo, too; she showed us the mound of earth at one end of the garden. It was only eight o'clock when she woke us up. She couldn't have slept at all.

She didn't say anything to Henri about what had happened after he had gone to sleep, so I kept quiet too. Henri looked drawn and tense; his eyes would keep wandering unhappily over the room as if he expected to see something bad, but didn't know what it would be. When we had finished the hot black coffee, he said, "Where's that damn boy?" "I don't think you'll be seeing Albert this morning," Miss Finney said enigmatically. She gathered up the cups and saucers and went back toward the kitchen.

"What did she mean by that?" Henri asked me.

"I don't know exactly," I said. "She has something up her sleeve. She's been acting mysterious ever since she made me turn around and come back yesterday." I hesitated, then decided to begin telling him. "A lot of things happened last night after you went to sleep, Henri," I said. "This business of Dodo was just the beginning. It's bad news and you'll have to—"

Miss Finney said quickly from the next room, "Bad news isn't the half of it. Shut up, Hoop." She came through the door and knifed me with a look. "I'll see that Henri is told the way I want him to be and at the right time," she said. "Come on— we're all going to the Boutegourdes'."

Henri didn't ask any questions, but followed us in a resigned and unquestioning manner, as if his worries were worse than any news Miss Finney was going to have for him. We stepped out into a staggering sun and started for the truck, but just as Henri was about to get in he said, "Wait a minute," and crossed back over the yard to the eagle. He pulled away a wooden pin and swung open one side of the cage. The bird dropped awkwardly from his perch to the floor, and waddled tentatively out into the open yard. His black crest rose and fell, and even from the truck I could see his big yellow eye blotted out as the colorless membrane slid back and forth over it. Henri stood still, watching. The bird left the ground with a leap and a heavy flapping of wings. It flew awkwardly into the air, more like a chicken than an eagle, and landed on the low branch of a tree at the edge of the bush, teetering uncertainly.

Henri threw the wooden peg into the empty cage and came over to the truck. "He'll get his wings back soon," he said, and the three of us crowded into the small cab so that after a minute our thighs were sticky and uncomfortable against one another's.

The air had the sullen weight of moist heat without breeze. The chirping and squawking of the birds hidden in the bush was subdued; the leaves hung still and the grass stood listlessly in the fields. The truck itself seemed sluggish as it churned along the road, and I became more and more aware of the abnormal quiet which had settled down over the station. Then I realized that the natives were gone.

Ordinarily they would have been cutting grass or trimming foliage, walking along the paths as they went about their errands, or sitting motionless in the shade. They were as much a part of the place as the hills or the clumps of bush, and without them the station was incomplete, hanging in the hot morning air through which we plowed as if through some viscous substance. None of us spoke, but sat side by side sweating until we drove up in front of the Boutegourdes' house and I switched off the motor. Its sound died out and the stillness closed against us.

We found Papa Boutegourde and Miss Collins sitting dumbly in the front room, both dressed now, but Papa's face looking heavy and puffy, and Miss Collins' eyes red and grainy from weariness. They said Jacqueline was still in bed, and that Madame Boutegourde and Gabrielle were in their rooms packing. Madame Boutegourde would not stay, and would not let Gabrielle stay on that station an hour longer than could be helped. They were driving to Costermansville as soon as they could pack some clothes and a lunch. "They might as well go," said Miss Finney. Everybody took it for granted she was in charge. Papa Boutegourde looked too old and bewildered to do anything but follow orders. "Somebody has to go and report this business anyhow. We've got a lot to do today, César. I don't suppose any of your boys showed up this morning, did they?"

Papa Boutegourde shook his head.

Miss Finney said, "Henri, sit down please." She turned to Papa Boutegourde. "César, let Angélique and Gabrielle get away whenever they can. They'll go to the administrator and he'll send somebody up here. Have you got a pistol? Give it to Angélique. She won't need it but she'll feel safer. I'm taking Hoop and we're going down to the village. I'm going to bring back some of those natives. They've got a grave to dig." She went on talking to Papa Boutegourde but turned her glance on Henri. He looked at her in a quiet, stupefied way. "We'll have to bury the body. Find me a piece of canvas to wrap it in; if we have to dig it up again it'll be in better condition than if we let it lie around. We'll photograph it. I've got the laboratory locked and I don't want anybody poking around there. That leaves you four here—César and Henri and Emily and Jacqueline. Jacqueline can stay in bed as long as she wants to, but I want your word that you won't separate for a minute, not even in pairs. Do you get all that?"

"I've got it, Mary," said Miss Collins.

"I'll say good-by to Angélique," said Miss Finney, and went out of the room. We sat there without talking until she came back. "Come on, Hoop," she said. She turned to Henri. "They'll tell you about it," she said, and we started out the door.

"Mary!" cried Miss Collins, "hadn't you better take—"

"I won't need a gun," said Miss Finney. "Come on, Hoop."

❄ ❄ ❄

We drove as far as we could in the truck and then began the long walk down the snaking path to the village. Mary Finney was a good walker. We went along steadily and at a sensible pace, single file. It was hard to talk and Miss Finney wasn't feeling communicative anyway.

"What are you taking me into?" I asked once.

"Nothing that's going to hurt you," she said. "I think I've got this whole thing figured out but I'm not ready to tell you yet."

"Tell me now," I said.

"Not now," said Miss Finney, "but you can be the first to know. I won't tell 'til I'm ready."

I said, "It's not a comfortable feeling, walking into their territory this way."

"I know what I'm doing," she said. "You'll be all right as long as they see you're with me." She took a few steps in silence and then said, "It all adds up to an awful total, Hoopie."

"You can't be trying to tie in this M'buku business, last night and all, with what happened in Bafwali!" I said.

"I tell you I've got it tied in already," she said.

"What do you know that I don't know?" I asked. "What have you found out in the way of—figures, that you haven't told me?"

"Nothing," she said. "A lot of what I know you told me. The rest you saw as well as I did."

"I don't know what you're talking about."

"You're a nice kid, Hoopie," Mary Finney told me, "but you're blind as a bat. I'll tell you when it's time."

I had to let it go at that until we got to the village.

It was a miserable affair, two rows of thatched huts, circular, with conical roofs, and all around them the earth had been beaten to dust by the natives' feet. They had kept the bush chopped away for about fifty feet on each side of the village area, but then a tangle of low growth began, gradually rising into the tall trees and hanging lianas of full forest. We stopped at the edge of the first row of huts and stood looking along the squalid alleyway.

The sun was blazing down and the air felt compressed between the hills that rose on every side. The dust we had stirred up hung around our ankles, wavering gently, but outside of that there wasn't a sign of anything moving, nor a sound, except what we could hear of the perpetual whispering and peeping of the forest.

"There's nobody here," I said.

"Oh yes there is," said Miss Finney. "Look over there." She pointed to a hut about midway along the stretch of village. There was something sitting on the ground on the shady side. "Too old to take along," Miss Finney said, and started forward. I followed her until we got up close to the old woman.

She was certainly the ugliest of all God's forsaken creatures. Her skin was like something smoked and dried and flaky with ashes, covered with the grayish scale you find on all old natives. She was only a sack for her twisted old bones, with a heavy load of entrails settled into the bottom of it, and strange, badly padded appendages for arms and legs. She looked up at us with a sick monkey face and blinked her eyes once, slowly. That was all. She was sick and old, but she must have had behind her a good record in child-bearing, with the respect and the worldly goods that come with it, for in addition to the standard beaten-bark G-string, she had accumulated during her lifetime an armband of tinny metal eight or nine inches wide, and four or five strings of bright glass beads that hung around her neck with plenty of amulets and one large heavy metal pendant. Her G-string held a long shiny knife over the withered hump that had been her right buttock, and she supported a clay pipe in one hand. As we watched her she gathered enough energy to lift it ever so slowly to her mouth, and to take ever so slow a puff. Her arm fell back then, and to all outward appearances she died and froze squatting there. She had big white skewers in her ears. There was a dark spot moving out of the next hut now, like something sub-animal, and as naked, but recognizable as another female. When I moved toward it, it stopped and sank down on its haunches. I pulled a coin out of my pocket, a small one with a hole in the center, and held it out to her. Like a piece of leather coming to life she raised her eyelids, and finally she raised her hand. It was covered with raw white spots. I dropped the coin into it and she looked at it without expression. Her fingers oozed into a fist over the coin and she remained squatting there, blinking in the light. "There'll be a few more in the huts," Miss Finney said, "all just like these." She stood in the dust in the middle of the village, looking around every which way. After the first glance she didn't pay any more attention to the two hunks of dormant flesh. She put her hands on her hips and shook her head and said, "They've sure cleared out. This is just like old times."

She took a deep breath and cupped both hands to her mouth, and called through them, a few bizarre syllables, in the direction of the bush. We stood there listening, but everything remained quiet.

"They've had the living daylights scared out of them," she said. "They'll do it every time—or used to. Used to be, every time we showed up we'd find the villages deserted, just like this. That was a long time ago, though. Only time I've seen it since those days was during the rebellion."

After a few moments she called again, a long loud hornlike call. She waited halfheartedly, apparently not really expecting an answer, and then turned to me.

"You'll have to leave, Hoop," she said. "I don't stand a dog's chance of getting them out while you're here. They're not very far in. They're watching us right now. I'll be back at the station as soon as I can make it."

"You can't stay here alone, in the middle of this ring of savages," I said. "I'm going to stay."

She smiled, a very good smile, wide, pleased, and friendly, but she said, "If they were going to hurt us we'd have been cut into slivers by now. I'll see you later. Remember every word everybody says, and don't let any two of them get together alone."

"You're the boss," I said, and turned to go, but she called me back suddenly and said, "Hoopie, have you got a handkerchief?" I reached into the hip pocket where I always carry one, but it was gone.

"I thought not," said Miss Finney. "Think that one over." She grinned and I knew she was teasing me about something but I didn't know what.

"I hope you're having a lot of fun," I said. "I'll have the truck waiting for you."

As I mounted the path I turned to look back at her. She had moved over to the shade and was sitting on a log drum at the side of a hut, fanning herself with her helmet. I could almost feel the natives moving cautiously to the edge of the bush as I left the village behind me, but all the way back to the limits of the station, and then through the station grounds to the Boutegourdes', I didn't see a soul.

Miss Finney arrived about an hour after I did. She had the back of the truck full of natives and said some of the house boys were coming on foot. The boys in the truck got out and huddled in a group, their eyes wide and white, watching Miss Finney as if their lives depended on not losing sight of her.

# CHAPTER SIX

## —or Parties Unknown

I DON'T KNOW EXACTLY when it was that I began to see that Miss Finney was intent on tightening the ring of circumstance around Henri. But even when I got to the point where I was willing to admit to myself that Henri was mixed up in the business somehow, or at least knew something he was hiding, the puzzling thing was still why anybody would want to kill the de l'Andréneau brothers at all. I couldn't make head nor tail of the things that happened, and if it was all part of a worked-out scheme, the scheme seemed too complicated to be reasonable. On the other hand it was simple enough at its face value, André having died of amoebic dysentery, and a couple of weeks later an entirely unconnected event, Gérôme's death at the hands of the M'bukus, their revenge for his having hanged one of them. Revenge isn't a common motive for premeditated murder among civilized people, story books to the contrary, but it's the commonest one among primitive ones.

But Miss Finney insisted that anybody with eyes in his head wouldn't be fooled, and she didn't consider for a minute that the natives had anything to do with it. It is hard from this distance to understand why any of us were fooled, but in the time that has elapsed, the things that were actually connected with the murders have stuck with me, while other impressions have faded. And of course after you once know the straight of anything you wonder how you could have thought anything else.

I've already told Henri's story—that he had fallen asleep in his clothes around eight o'clock and had slept until he had been awakened to find Dodo, just as Miss Finney and I came up.

As for the rest of them, Miss Collins had had a light supper with the three Boutegourdes and they had all sat around for a while in the living room. Then at about eight o'clock she had said good night and gone to bed. She had read her Bible for half an hour, as she did every night, and then had gone to sleep and slept soundly until she had been awakened by all the rumpus in the living room. When she came in, Papa and Madame Boutegourde were lifting Jacqueline up off the floor where she had fallen into the room, and were laying her out on the couch. I had arrived a few minutes later.

Papa and Madame Boutegourde said that after Miss Collins had gone to bed at eight o'clock, they had stayed up playing a few hands of piquet for another hour, and then they had gone to bed too. They had slept until Jacqueline came screaming into the house.

All this was simple enough, but Gabrielle's story was more complicated. She had been moping around all evening, seeming restless and unhappy, and when Madame Boutegourde was ready for bed she told Gabrielle that she had better go to bed too, and reminded her that she had had a headache that morning. Gabrielle said she wasn't sleepy, because she had been kept in bed until noon. She laid out a table of solitaire with the cards Papa and Madame Boutegourde had been playing with, and promised her mother that she would go to bed after a few hands. She didn't go to bed, though; she played solitaire until she couldn't stand it any longer, she said, then she decided she would smoke a cigarette. She didn't ordinarily smoke so she didn't carry cigarettes, but Papa Boutegourde always had some. She slipped into her parents' bedroom and found the cigarettes in her father's shirt pocket. Papa Boutegourde was snoring lightly and Madame was breathing evenly by his side. When Miss Finney told Gabrielle that it was important for her to remember absolutely everything, Gabrielle knotted her brows for a minute and said, "Well, then, if it makes any difference, I forgot to get Papa's matches, and I was afraid I might wake them if I went in again so soon, so I went back to the kitchen for a match and lit my cigarette there." She told her whole story in similar detail. She had to pass Miss Collins's door on the way to the kitchen. It was open to get the cross-draft but she didn't look in. "Why should I?" she said. She came back through the house and went out onto the front porch to smoke. She turned out all the lights because it was a pretty night and she wanted to feel alone, and she felt more alone outside and in the dark. She had sat down on the steps for a while, but there were so many mosquitoes that she had got up, and paced up and down the porch. It was a very small porch, and as she told her story I had the picture of her, tense and distraught, taking the few steps the length of the porch, then turning, taking a few steps, turning, and always puffing on the cigarette in the fast uneasy way she had of smoking. The mosquitoes were so bad that even walking didn't keep them off her legs, so she threw the cigarette away and went back into the house. Just then she heard a car in the distance; she had glanced at the clock as she turned on the living-room light, but she didn't remember the exact time—it was a little after ten, she thought.

She knew the car must be Jacqueline getting back, and this made her feel worse than ever. She felt lonesome, and wanted company so much that she started back to wake Miss Collins, but she thought better of it and returned to the living room. The sound of the car had died away; she knew Jacqueline was at Gérôme's by now, and she hated the thought of having to be around her again. Then she did something that she frequently did, she said, that she had learned from Jeannette while she was alive. Jeannette used to memorize poetry to occupy herself when she was unhappy or restless, and she had taught Gabrielle to do it. Gabrielle went to her own room and picked out an anthology that Jeannette had given her. She memorized a verse by Guillaume Apollinaire:

> Je passais au bord de la Seine
> Un livre ancien sous le bras
> Le fleuve est pareil à ma peine
> Il s'écoule et ne tarit pas
> Quand donc finira la semaine

It was a sad, quiet little verse and made her feel better, but it took only a few minutes to memorize, and she had begun on a sonnet by Louise Labé:

> Baise m'encor, rebaise moy et baise:
> Donne m'en un de tes plus savoureus,
> Donne m'en un de tes plus amoureus:

This one hadn't gone so well, and she had flung the book down and decided to try to get some sleep after all. She lay in bed unable to do anything but think, and although she didn't say so, I could imagine what she was thinking about, mulling it all over in her head about the night before. Finally she got up and put on her clothes again and went out. She said she had been moving around so much that night that she was afraid she might have disturbed her parents, and so she slipped out of her window instead of going through the front room again.

She had gone out to the promontory.

"Why *there*?" asked Madame Boutegourde, while Gabrielle was telling this.

"For the view," said Gabrielle. "The grass fires were pretty."

She had told all this calmly enough, but she had all she could do to keep from going to pieces as she told the rest of it. She had sat there for a while, she didn't know how long, until she had heard the sound of someone coming. She had run back into the edge of the bush, and had seen one figure come out onto the promontory, bent over under the weight of what he carried on his back. He had thrown his weight onto the ground. The body was long and thin and in white pants and shirt; she knew it was Gérôme. She could see the other figure in not much more than silhouette, but she could tell it was a native. She had shut her eyes when she saw that he had a knife, and what he was doing to the body; she was afraid she would faint, and concentrated everything on staying conscious and quiet. She didn't know how long it took until the native left, going down the path into the valley, toward the village; she didn't remember how long it had taken her to go back along the path when she saw my light in the distance. She thought it was a native, with a light he had stolen. She had told him not to touch her, and then had recognized me when I turned the flash on myself. She showed me Gérôme's body, as I have told, and I took her back to her house, where Miss Finney was still trying to get something besides gibberish out of Jacqueline.

When I told them that I had found Gérôme, and that he was dead, Jacqueline went into violent hysterics again and Miss Finney had to give her a hypodermic right away. But Miss Finney told Gabrielle that she had to keep hold of herself long enough to tell exactly what had happened. While Miss Collins put Jacqueline to bed, Gabrielle told us her story as I've just set it down. It was hard for her to do, and you could see her hanging onto herself for dear life near the end of it, but it was Madame Boutegourde who finally gave way and had to be attended to next by Miss Finney.

I didn't have anything to add to all this. As I've said, we spent the rest of that night moving Gérôme's body into the laboratory, until Miss Finney and I had gone back to Henri's. Miss Finney only asked me one question.

"Hoop," she said, as we drove down to Henri's, "what exactly did Gaby say, when you flashed that light on her?"

"Just what she said she said," I told her. "She just kept saying, *Don't touch me, don't touch me,* over and over again."

"Those her exact words?"

"You asked me, I told you. Yes."

"Strange," said Miss Finney. "If she didn't know it was you, why did she speak in English?"

I felt myself flushing in the dark. "Sorry," I said. "She did say it in French, now that I think of it."

"Damnit," said Miss Finney, "when I say exact words, I mean exact words."

"All right then, her exact words were *Ne me touchez pas.*"

"The next time I ask you a question, see that you answer it correctly the first time," said Miss Finney.

"Yes, ma'am," I agreed.

It wasn't until Gabrielle and Madame Boutegourde had left the next morning for Costermansville that Miss Finney set about the job of getting Jacqueline out of bed and getting her story in rational form. Jacqueline had a field day. If the shades of Bernhardt and Rachel and all the other girls who have their portraits in the lobbies of the *Comédie-Française* were listening in, they must have been awe-struck.

In the first place, after doing a good job on the breakfast-lunch that Miss Finney and Miss Collins took in to her on a tray, Jacqueline said she simply could not go on, simply could not, until she had had a chance to freshen up in her own room. Miss Finney wanted the story at Gérôme's anyway, where the thing had happened, so she and Jacqueline and I went down there. Papa Boutegourde and Henri and Miss Collins stayed behind. Some of the natives Miss Finney had brought back with her were getting a grave dug. It turned out that there was no film on the station, so photographs were out, but Papa

Boutegourde and Henri had agreed to sew the body in the canvas, and we would all see that it was properly buried that afternoon, with Miss Collins reading a burial service. In the meanwhile Miss Finney would get Jacqueline's story. Henri and Papa Boutegourde looked surprised when Miss Finney said I was to come along with her, but nobody said anything.

Jacqueline had a hard time being a tragic figure on the way down to her house. She had asked for lipstick and mascara with her lunch tray, but either there was none in the house or Miss Finney had maliciously lied about it, so Jacqueline had to make her first entrance in the torn and bedraggled red crêpe pajamas without make-up. It added easily five years to her looks, and while her pallor was real enough it was only unhealthy, not dramatic.

After we got to Gérôme's, she kept Miss Finney and me waiting close to three quarters of an hour while she "freshened up." Miss Finney poked her nose into everything in the living room and then looked over the hallway and all the other rooms not within Jacqueline's hearing. Nothing but the living room was messed up. The throw-rugs were rumpled on the waxed concrete floor, and although two brandy glasses were standing upright on the table, the open brandy bottle had overturned and the room was filled with its sharp, grapy smell. While I smoked cigarettes and watched her, Miss Finney finished our period of waiting by going around and around the living room like a bumblesome old dog trying to search out a bone. She would mutter under her breath and I got the idea that most of what she said was pretty uncomplimentary to our hostess.

It was a shame that there were only the two of us to see Jacqueline's second entrance. She appeared in the doorway and stood there quietly for a brave moment. She had creamed and powdered away the last signs of the disfiguring bruise on her mouth, and had substituted a dark, subdued lipstick for the flaming vermilion she usually wore. There were faint, faint shadows in the hollows of her cheeks, and her great, sad eyes looked out with courage from her romantically pallid face. Her hair was parted in the middle and brushed back simply. She looked young and fragile, and the black lace negligée she had assumed in her new widowhood was just about as funereal as a night with a nautch dancer. Miss Finney was never one to deny credit where credit was due. "Boy!" she said in genuine admiration. "Ain't that sumpin'!"

Jacqueline ignored this vulgarity and spoke her opening line with quiet fortitude.

"I am ready," she said.

"If you aren't, no woman ever was," snapped Miss Finney. "Let's get down to business."

Jacqueline met this with the patient smile of one whose grief lifted her above Miss Finney's coarse-grained nature. She set her body into motion and crossed over to a chair and sat down quietly, her hands folded in her lap.

"What do you want to know?" she asked.

I could see Miss Finney choking back whatever comment first occurred to her. She took a moment to compose herself and then said directly and without rancor, "I want to know everything just as it happened, Jacqueline. You tried to tell us some of it last night but you never managed to make anything clear. I hope it won't be too painful for you to go over it again."

"Thank you," said Jacqueline piteously, "oh, thank you! I shall try."

She had reached the station, she said, a little after ten o'clock. She was tired, but happy to be coming back to Gérôme to sustain him during his period of grief for his brother. Gérôme was waiting for her; he had stayed up, he said, on the bare chance that she might be able to make it that night. It had been a sweet homecoming. Sad, of course, because of André's death, but joyous too, because—

Jacqueline lowered her eyes, looking at her hands in her lap. "I am telling you everything, Mademoiselle Finney," she said. "I know you do not like me, and it is true I was not always a good wife to Gérôme." She raised her eyes again and looked into Miss Finney's with simple candor. She spoke with such apparent sincerity that I felt shamefaced for being unable to believe her. "I was selfish," she said. "I was spoiled. Paris and beautiful things had been my life, my whole life. I love beauty. I love gaiety, Mademoiselle Finney. Here in this wilderness I was lost, imprisoned. I—"

She rose and clenched her hands at her sides, and turned her back to us suddenly. The back of the negligée was just as effective as the front. When she had modeled it for a moment she turned to us with tears in her eyes and in her voice. "I became cross. I was not always kind to Gérôme. I will tell you the truth. I had gone to Léopoldville because I had told Gérôme I could stand it no longer. He told me to go to Léopoldville for a vacation and think things over."

There had been a great reconciliation. She had told him that the time away from him had given her the opportunity to see things in their true perspective. She loved him, she wanted only to be with him, to be a good wife. If it meant she must stay in the wilderness, his wilderness should be her wilderness; their wilderness, she said, would be their own little world. There had been tears, tears of joy mixed with those of sorrow for André.

All this was beginning to stretch out, but Miss Finney was patient.

"Why, I'm very happy for you, Jacqueline," she said awkwardly. "Maybe you'd better tell the rest as briefly as you can. You don't want to tax your strength."

"Thank you," said Jacqueline tremulously. "Thank you, dear friend."

Gérôme had suggested a little drink, some very special brandy he had been saving for their next wedding anniversary. She was tired, desperately tired, but this was an occasion. While Gérôme had gone after the brandy, she had gone to freshen up and to slip into the red crêpe lounging pajamas, favorites of Gérôme's. This had taken her some little time, she said, and it was easy for us to believe it. When she had come back into the room, Gérôme was standing petrified by the table with the brandy on it, facing two natives she had never seen before (but she knew none of the natives, hardly her own houseboys, even; they all looked alike, these savages). She had not heard them come in, she had heard no sound at all; they had simply appeared out of thin air, and she had entered to face the terrifying tableau in the living room. She pointed out the spots where the natives were standing, where Gérôme was standing, and the door she had come in—the same one she had just now entered.

Gérôme spoke to the natives in French, asking them what they wanted. They had answered briefly in their own tongue, probably saying that they did not understand French, perhaps making some demand. Neither Jacqueline nor Gérôme knew a word of the language.

Jacqueline remembered Gérôme's pistol in their bedroom. She turned to leave the room but one of the natives was upon her in an instant, grabbing her from behind by the arms near the shoulder, and making the bruises Madame Boutegourde had seen last night. Gérôme had turned to attack the native. The second native jumped across the room and felled Gérôme with one blow. Gérôme lay still on the concrete floor. Jacqueline had screamed. The second native stepped over Gérôme's body and grabbed both her wrists in one hand. "He was big, big! A great black brute of a thing—" and she displayed to us her two small bruised wrists that he had clamped in his one great hand. He had put the other over her mouth. She had fainted.

When she came to, both natives had Gérôme's body and were carrying it out of the room. She had crawled across the floor toward them on her hands and knees. Then rising to her knees she had beat at one of them with her fists. He freed one hand and hit her in the mouth, saying something in his language. She didn't know how long she was unconscious that time. When she came to she was alone. She was half crazy with terror; she hadn't even remembered that she could have driven the car. She had run all the way to the Boutegourdes', falling down, running into bushes. She remembered it only as one remembers a nightmare. The Boutegourdes' screen was unlatched; she had managed to get into the room, calling for help, and had collapsed.

Jacqueline did a fine job on this recitation. It was one that would have been easy to overplay, which was even difficult not to overplay. But she did it just right, with only occasional gestures, and those all the more effective for being quickly stifled, letting her tone of voice and the attitude of her body, stiffening or wilting, do the rest. The script was terrible, like anything an actress writes for herself to play, but even Bergner couldn't have got more out of it.

Miss Finney listened thoughtfully and attentively to all of this. When it was over, she had only one comment:

"Yeh," she said.

❋ ❋ ❋

Miss Finney and I left the house and started back to the Boutegourdes'.

"Well," she said, "what'd you think of all that?"

"I'd like to have the stubs," I said.

She shot me a suspicious glance. "What stubs?" she asked.

"The ticket stubs," I said. "For my memory book."

"Oh," said Miss Finney. "You're not very funny. You're right, though—she certainly played that one right up to the hilt. How much of it do you believe?"

"I don't know," I said, "but I wouldn't say it was one hundred per cent autobiographical. You probably don't believe any of it."

"Oh yes I do," Miss Finney said. "I believe she ran all the way to the Boutegourdes' so she could arrive out of breath and all messed up. But the word hasn't been invented that would say what I think of the rest of it."

"You don't believe anybody," I said. "You keep telling me I have to watch out for these false faces and stuff. How about you and your own face value?"

Miss Finney looked a little bit smug. "I'm pretty good at fooling people when I want to," she said, "but I haven't fooled you much, Hoopie. I've teased you and I've held out on you and I've sneaked into Henri's room while you were asleep and stolen your handkerchief out of your hind pocket, but I never have deliberately fooled you."

The meanest thing I could do to Mary Finney was to fail to rise to the bait, so I began whistling *Love in Bloom* under my breath and let my glance wander around vacantly. She stood it for about four bars and then said, "Oh, shut up! *You're* not fooling *me*."

"All right then," I said. "I'm wild to know about the hand-kerchief. I'm wild to know about all the rest of this business too but I'm not going to sit up and beg for any of it."

"I'll tell you some of it after the funeral," she said. "You're a fine, patient boy, Hoopie, and your Aunt Mary is getting very fond of you. By the way, while you were waiting for me to get back from the village, did anybody say anything or do anything?"

"No," I said. "We just sat around. I don't know about the others, but I sat there wondering whether you would yell very much when they began giving you the works down in the village."

"They'd have to get awfully hungry before they'd go after a tough old piece like me," Miss Finney said. "So nobody said anything? Well, that's all right, everything fits in anyhow."

When we reached the Boutegourdes', Miss Collins was there alone. She had some cool lemonade fixed up for us and while we were drinking it Henri and Papa Boutegourde came in. They looked a sickish color but said the body was sewed up in the canvas and loaded on the station truck, and that we could bury it any time now. Papa Boutegourde said he would go get Jacqueline. I was sorry that she was going to come on again, because anything short of her appearing in a clap of thunder would be an anticlimax, but Jacqueline must have felt the same way, because Papa Boutegourde came back without her and said that she didn't feel equal to seeing Gérôme buried in the

sordid way it would have to be done. So we took him out to
the field and buried him not far from André. It was a dismal
business. Miss Collins read the service in a small wispy voice,
but without hesitation and somehow impressively, although she
looked like a little bunch of faggots tied up in a rag as she stood
there in the hot sun in the big field. Neither André nor Gérôme
had meant anything much to me one way or another, but as the
natives began filling Gérôme's grave, so near the fresh mound
of his brother's, I felt depressed beyond measure. It was all so
meager and so desolate, the two de l'Andréneaus buried inglo-
riously in an open field on the station which had gone to pieces
in their hands. What would happen to the Company now, I
wondered. Probably Papa Boutegourde would be appointed
director of the station, find some kind of help, and go on with
all the cards stacked against him, a good man in a bad spot. I
thought of Gabrielle and Madame Boutegourde, well on their
way to Costermansville by now, and I hoped they would find a
way never to come back to the Congo-Ruzi.

When we came back from the funeral, Miss Finney said to
all of us, "Anybody scared?"

Everyone made negative murmurs.

"Well, I don't think anybody has any reason to be," she
said. "I guess nobody has any doubts as to what happened.
Jacqueline says there were two natives and Gabrielle only saw
one, but there could be explanations for that. Down in the
village they don't know anything about it and I believe them.
I'm convinced of it and I'll stake my life on it."

"You may be staking all our lives on it, Mary," Miss Collins
said.

"All right, then," said Miss Finney cheerfully, "all your
lives. I tell you our village doesn't know anything about it.
These natives came from another village. This wasn't a rebellion, either; it was personal revenge, some male relative of the
M'buku Gérôme hanged. That's why he mutilated the body
that way. No point in getting your revenge and not getting
credit for it; that's what a native wants out of revenge, to show

he's avenged the family honor, not just the personal satisfaction of it. This native or these natives, whichever it was, came from the same village as those who killed the subadministrator. He's not interested in us and he's trotting along some bush path miles from here by now. We're safe." If Miss Finney wanted to string them along and make them believe she thought the natives did it, it was all right with me, but I said, "This village was bound to have known something about it, or why did they stay away from the station this morning?"

Not only Miss Finney, but everybody in the room, began to say the same thing—that the natives had their own grapevine and their own way of knowing what happened. You always hear the whites say this in the Congo, and I suppose it's true. Anyhow I let this one pass.

Miss Finney said, "We can't do anything until they send somebody up here from Costermansville. What does everybody want to do?"

Everybody wanted to rest.

Miss Finney said, "I could use a little peace and quiet myself. Henri, you go home and go to bed. I think you'll find Albert there by now; I talked to him down in the village. Hoop, you go to the guest house. Emily, you've got your own room here. I'll go to Gérôme's. Guess somebody ought to be with Jacqueline besides the house boys."

Miss Finney asked me to take her to Jacqueline's so she could leave the old rattletrap of a station wagon for Miss Collins in case she should need it. Henri got into his car and started off ahead of us. As we got near Jacqueline's he stopped and waved good-by to us. We waved back and he started up again and disappeared around a curve in the road. Miss Finney turned to me. "School's out, Hoopie," she said. "Let's go to the guest house."

"Don't you want to keep an eye on Jacqueline?"

"As long as everybody else thinks I'm at Jacqueline's, nobody's going to go there. And as long as Jacqueline thinks I'm hanging around everybody else, she's going to stay home. And anyway, come to think of it," she added, "I don't care who sees who, any more. You got any whisky in your bag?" I had.

"I don't drink before nightfall very often," she said, "but I've got one coming today. Come on. Let's talk." We drew up to the guest house and went in. I brought my bag from the back of the truck and we mixed a couple of bush highballs—whisky with chlorinated water and no ice—pretty bad the first few times, but you get used to it, and we certainly needed them that afternoon.

❀ ❀ ❀

The single room of the guest house was very small. Miss Finney sat on the bed, because it was more comfortable than the stiff chair where I sat. She sat there with her drink in her hand and after the first few swallows she began to sag and look tired.

"Do you feel all right?" I asked.

"No," she said wearily, "I feel pretty bad. I'm a woman fifty years old, Hoopie. I'm a little overweight and I've always been homely, and I didn't get to bed last night. That's enough to depress anybody."

"I'm sorry," I said. "You've been acting so bright and chipper."

"I know," Miss Finney said. "I've been cracking *pretty wise*. Ever hear of whistling in the dark, Hoopie?"

I told her I had done lots of it from time to time.

"Me too," she said, "but never so much as I've done the last twenty-four hours. I've tried to stand off and figure things out impersonally. It's been fun, the *figuring out*. It's the answer that's got me whistling."

"Me too," I said, "if it's what I think it is."

She raised her eyebrows in a question.

I said, "I don't know how you figure things, but you've got Henri tied up in it some way and I like Henri."

"The trouble with you, Hoopie," Miss Finney said, "is that you admire good looks too much."

"Maybe," I admitted. I knew it was true. I changed the subject. "You're not infallible yourself. I caught you in a mistake. The knife."

She looked blank for a moment and then straightened out of her slouch and said, "Oh my gosh!"

"All this rigmarole you gave them up at the Boutegourdes' about it being a native from another village. It didn't explain how that knife of Gérôme's got there. It didn't fool Papa Boutegourde."

"You two found the knife when you moved Gérôme. Did you tell Henri or Emily or anybody else?"

"I didn't mention it to anybody myself. I can't vouch for Papa Boutegourde."

Miss Finney shrugged and sagged again. "It doesn't make any difference," she said, "whether I fooled anybody or not. I was only making a gesture."

I said, "How about straightening me out on a few things?" I filled our glasses with a second round of weak drinks, just to have something to sip. Miss Finney said:

"You've got what looks like a bunch of disconnected and irrational circumstances connected with these two killings, and with the life on this station in general. The way to go about straightening them out is to set your imagination to working and see what you can invent in the way of some single circumstance that will explain away a lot of the others. The more it explains away, the more likely your invention is to be true. See?"

"Yes, but I don't see what you invented."

She began to perk up again as she started rehashing her figuring-out.

"Well, look," she said. "There were a lot of things that didn't make sense one at a time, much less in a group, without the one unknown that would tie them together. I'm sure Jacqueline fed André the dysentery culture in Bafwali; she could have slipped it in his bedside carafe, for instance. But why in the world should she want to kill him? That had to be explained; it didn't make sense. There was something else about Jacqueline, too—all of a sudden after she came here she took an unexplained dislike to Henri. She wouldn't go anywhere he was, or let him in her house. Nobody could say why, not even Henri. And you know enough about Jacqueline to realize that ordinarily she'd have been out tooth and nail for a rich piece of flesh like that one, especially with nothing else in sight but André and Papa Boutegourde. And then Jeannette's books. Gabrielle said Henri must have put them away because they gave him more pain than comfort. You know he didn't put them away, he burnt them, but even so, Gabrielle's explanation for why he got rid of them might still have been offered. But it doesn't hold water. Jeannette's things should have brought Henri more and more pleasure and less and less pain as her death receded in the background, no matter how much Henri suffered when she first died. That was three years ago, so why did he burn the books all of a sudden, within the last few months at least since Gabrielle saw them there, or maybe even within the last few weeks?"

"And you've invented one circumstance that explains all those things," I said.

"Those and some others," Miss Finney said. "There's one circumstance I don't have to invent, though. Surely you know Gaby's in love with Henri? She wouldn't talk to you about him; when she was a kid she loved Jeannette and Henri the way she never had a chance to love anybody else. When Jeannette died, Gaby transferred all the affection she had for her right on over and added it to what she already had for Henri. And she never got a chance to know another man who could hold a candle to Henri, anyway not until you came along with your own feeble little light. She'd have been abnormal if she hadn't loved Henri. But the thing that needed explaining was why Henri never gave her a break. She was pretty and young and good, cut out to be the best kind of wife. There was the emotional tie-up with Jeannette, too, and that kind of thing happens over and over again—the widower marries his dead wife's sister or best friend and so on. And Henri's the kind of man who needs women the way he needs to breathe, and is attracted to them with as natural a reflex as his breathing action. Well, why not to Gaby? I'm sure he was fond of her but nothing ever happened, and she was the only woman around here after Jeannette died."

"For a few months. Until Jacqueline came."

"That's hitting the nail on the head," said Miss Finney. "Henri and Jacqueline are lovers. They've been lovers for a couple of years."

"*What?*"

Miss Finney sighed. "Of course they are. Use your noggin, Hoop." She took a long swallow of her drink and looked tired. "I wish this thing had some ice in it," she said.

"But Jacqueline didn't like Henri," I babbled. "You just said so."

"That's one of the circumstances it explains," said Miss Finney. "Jacqueline and Henri got along all right when she and Gérôme first came here. He hung around their house all the time—Henri told you so himself. I don't know exactly when they became lovers, but it couldn't have been too long after Jacqueline arrived, not with the kind of campaign she must have waged. Don't argue with me that Henri would have stayed true to Jeannette's memory. He really loved his wife, but the double standard was invented to take care of men like Henri. He'd had the habit of visceral relaxation probably ever since he sprouted his first whisker; he'd even have found it a release from his grief over Jeannette. The mere act of love doesn't count as an infidelity with Henri's kind, and I'm not sure that it should. I said I don't know when this business with Jacqueline began, but if I had the date when she first complained to Gérôme that she didn't like Henri Debuc and didn't want to be around him any more than could be helped, I'd be willing to bet I could place the time of their first brangle within twenty-four hours. Didn't like Henri my foot. Just a cover up."

"It explains about Gabrielle," I said.

"Sure," said Miss Finney. "If Jacqueline hadn't shown up I think the chances would have been a hundred to one that Henri would have worked around to marrying Gaby after a decent interval. It couldn't happen as soon as a thing like this Jacqueline business did, because with Gabrielle it would have been something more than this sort of emptying process that went on with that hussy. All right, wince. I'm crude, but I know the psycho-biology of the Henris. He wouldn't have pulled any funny stuff with a nice girl like Gabrielle; Henri's too honest."

I winced again.

"I didn't mean it that way, Hoopie," Miss Finney said quickly. "I understand how it happened between you two. Look, are you feeling any more sensible? About marrying Gaby, I mean?"

"That's not what we're talking about," I said. "So you think Henri couldn't fall in love with Gabrielle while Jacqueline had her hooks in him."

"I didn't mean that exactly," she said. "Lots of men have fallen legitimately in love with a good woman while they had a bad one on the side. But I imagine Henri got in beyond his depth before long. With things as tight as they are on this station, you can imagine what a stink that nymphomaniac female ham would have raised if she had seen Henri look twice at Gabrielle. Even with all the experience Jacqueline has behind her, I doubt if she's ever found anything so completely to her liking as Henri is, or anything she's so determined to hang on to. She isn't getting any younger, as the wise old saying goes. She'd have torn this station to pieces, even if she had to bring it down on her own head."

"And it explains what else?" I asked, although I was beginning to see things fit into place.

"It explains why she did away with André," Miss Finney said. "You know the degree of privacy there is around here. Even with the convention that nobody goes to anybody else's house without being asked, it was difficult and dangerous for

Henri and Jacqueline to meet. Gérôme was always going on those trips to the plantations, but even so, André still lived in the house. Sometimes they were both away at once and that must have been pretty nice, but you can imagine the dodging around and slipping in and out that must have gone on the rest of the time—Jacqueline down to Henri's or both of them to the guest house, and so on. I'll bet there wasn't a native around the place that didn't know what was going on, but they'd never tell. But you can't get away with it forever, and my guess is that once when Gérôme was away they got careless or had bad luck, and André got the goods on his brother's wife."

"Blackmail," I said.

"André wouldn't be above it," Miss Finney admitted, "and everybody knows that the mortality rate among blackmailers is awful high. I don't know what he was asking. I doubt it was money."

"Henri was dead broke," I said.

"Maybe that was why," she said. "But I'm thinking about how Jacqueline met André in Bafwali. You say he didn't know she was in the house. On the other hand, maybe she was waiting for him there while he was waiting for her down there at the Airways house where you saw him—that's where the plane passengers to Léopoldville spend the night. Maybe they got fouled up on making connections." She spoke bitterly and said, "Knowing my one and only ex-lover as I did, I wouldn't put it beyond him to have blackmailed Henri for money, and Jacqueline for another commodity she was in a position to supply."

"You certainly think a lot of your fellow human beings," I said.

"I've *seen* a lot of my fellow human beings, Emily dear," Miss Finney said. That one shut me up.

"Not that I think Jacqueline ever meant to give in," Miss Finney continued. "She agreed to the bargain with no intention of keeping it—not for moral reasons, that's Jacqueline's own particular little blind spot—but for reasons of distaste and security. She probably staved him off somehow in Bafwali and counted on the water carafe to settle things for her. Which it did."

"And you think Henri gave her the culture."

"I've tried to think not. I've tried to believe she stole it from the laboratory, but I can't come around to it. I think that was when Henri burnt the books. I think that when the whole thing passed into such a desperate phase instead of the casual byplay he thought it was going to be, he wanted to break every connection between Jeannette and himself, as if he might be dirtying her. Henri's a good man."

"If he gave Jacqueline those bugs, he's a murderer. You're calling him a good man and a murderer in the same breath."

"Yes."

"That can't be."

"All right then," said Miss Finney patiently, "he was a bad man. My God, Hoop, does everything have to be black or white to you? You can be good and bad at the same time; everybody is."

"Not that bad."

"Everybody doesn't get so badly involved," Miss Finney said. "Let's not argue it. What have I explained? Why Jacqueline claimed to dislike Henri, why Henri didn't pay any attention to Gaby, why he burnt Jeannette's books, and why Jacqueline had a motive for killing André. Had I mentioned anything else?"

"Not yet," I said.

"Fill my glass," Miss Finney told me, "and make it weak." I poured the drinks and Miss Finney said "Thanks" and took a sip of hers. "I'm dog-tired, Hoopie," she said. "I wish this were all over."

"What are you going to do?"

"I'm going to tell Henri."

My drink splashed over onto my hand. "So he can get away!" I said, and realized how much I wanted him to. Miss Finney moved her free hand in a gesture of half-amusement. "Can you imagine making a getaway from here?" she asked.

"How would you go about it? Where could you go, except Costermansville? You go the other way and the road peters out in a few native trading villages. And you know what Costermansville is, just how much chance you'd have of getting in and out of there without being noticed."

"But they could get there before the authorities knew about them."

"No difference. Costermansville's like any other Congo town. There's one road into it and there's one road out of it. There's the lake steamer, but it's even slower than the road and ends up at the same place, Kisenyi. Supposing they got to Kisenyi, or the other way, say to Usumbura? One road out and one road in, either place. Supposing they went to the next town after that? They could go all the way to Léopoldville for that matter. But the radio would catch up with them sooner or later. Hoopie, the Congo's as big as the United States from the Mississippi to the Atlantic, but white men travel through it on little threads of road and little trickles of water that just don't have any side-branches. If you were being hunted in the Congo you could no more get through it unobserved than you could cross Niagara Falls on a tight rope without people noticing. As for hiding out in the bush, that's a form of death in itself, and even if it weren't for us itinerant doctors and missionaries snooping around, any white man who tried to set himself up in a native village would be all over the Congo on the native grapevine so quick it would make your head swim. You can't get out of the Congo if they don't want you to, that's all."

"They could go by plane," I said, groping. "They could get into South Africa—or Kenya or Egypt. Cairo's big. They—"

"You know you're being silly," Miss Finney said. "Passports, for one thing. And with good luck you can get a plane reservation two weeks in advance without a priority, but it's more likely to be a month. And they don't give priorities on murder. They're stuck."

"Not if you don't report them," I said. "You only said you were going to tell Henri."

"Don't act so chickenhearted," Miss Finney said. "Those two are murderers."

"What makes you so sure about Henri?" I asked. "You're just guessing all this stuff. If nobody says anything they'll put it onto the natives."

"And hang a few of them for it," Miss Finney said. "However, I'm not going to report it. I'll tell you later what I'm going to do. But you're jumping the gun a little bit. I haven't said anything about Gérôme and the natives, I've just talked about André."

My eyes bugged out. "Do you mean you think maybe the natives did it after all?"

"Nothing of the kind," Miss Finney said.

"Then tell me about it. The way you figured it out."

Miss Finney looked uncertain and unhappy. "I can't figure that one out so completely, Hoop," she said. "I know some of it, but not all of it. I'm not sure we'll ever know it all. Why would you say they killed Gérôme?"

"Henri and Jacqueline? I wouldn't."

"They did. What would you say?"

I said, thinking it out as I went, "You're supposed to look for money in a civilized murder. Are there any more de l'Andréneau brothers or anybody?"

"No," Miss Finney said, "whatever is left of the Congo-Ruzi belongs to Jacqueline now."

"Then Henri and Jacqueline would have the money to get away. However bad off the Company is, if they sold everything they could get enough out of it to last them for a little while, to go somewhere, eventually to Belgium. It would last until they got started again."

Miss Finney shook her head. "That might work for Jacqueline, but not for Henri. He's not quite that cynical."

"You thought he was cynical enough to let Jacqueline have that dysentery culture."

Miss Finney waved away my interruption. "He wouldn't kill for a few dollars. No matter how broke he is, he's young and healthy and could always make a living. He certainly wouldn't murder for the privilege of running off with Jacqueline. If you ask me, he'd like to shake her. No. No on the money proposition."

"What makes you so sure he—they—killed Gérôme, then, if you haven't found a motive?"

"They over-clued," Miss Finney said. "It was silly to leave that knife there. Of course any native who had worked around Gérôme's house or office would know the knife and could get it. But it wasn't reasonable that any natives from our village would want to kill Gérôme, and even if they had, they wouldn't have had the sense of melodrama to kill with that knife. It isn't even a M'buku knife. Leaving that knife there was the silliest thing in the whole business. They must have been pretty well flustered by then. It makes you think maybe they didn't plan it ahead of time. The business of imitating the murder of the M'buku administrator was a desperate expedient in any case, but this knife—no, that's evidence against some white killer, not a black one."

"But why does the white killer have to be Henri?" I begged. "What are you doing with Gabrielle's story," I said, even feeling angry with Miss Finney now, "chucking it out the window? Good Lord, she saw the native! She saw him doing things to Gérôme's body, and she saw him leave on the path down to the village. Are you going to tell me Henri did this thing in blackface?"

"And," said Miss Finney, "when she saw you coming down the path with that light she thought it was another native and she said *Ne me touchez pas*. Exact words, remember?"

"Get to the point."

"My God, Hoop!" said Miss Finney. "She spoke in French. In *French*! Gabrielle never spoke to the natives in French. She was one of these Congo babies who have black boys for nursemaids and have to be spanked into speaking French. They always pick up Lingala first and they'd rather speak it; it's easier. She could tell all these native folk stories in their own tongue; she translates back and forth, the way she used to do for Jeannette, like a breeze. It was second nature to her to speak their own tongue to natives. Most of them wouldn't understand French anyhow. She didn't think you were a native—she thought you were a white man, a French-speaking white man. She didn't see a native out there with Gérôme—she saw a white man. She didn't see him go down the path to the village, she saw him go back in the direction of the station, the way he had come. When she saw that light bobbing through the bush she thought he was coming back for something, taking the short cut. When the light flashed on her she thought there was a murderer behind it. A white man! She didn't think it was a native. If she had, do you know what she'd have said? She'd have said *Koba! Kobadu bai! Koba-du bai!* My God, does that sound like *Ne me touchez pas* to you?"

"All right, all right," I said, feeling sick at what was coming next, but Miss Finney didn't hesitate.

"But then she pops up with this rigmarole about a native," she went on, "because she saw that white man and what he was doing to that body and she knew why he was doing it, and why he was laying him out on the path to the village like that. But she loved Henri. She might not have wanted him to touch her, not there in the bush or ever again, but she couldn't bring herself to give him away."

"It didn't have to be Henri!" I said. "It—there was someone else Gabrielle would have protected, another white man. Why couldn't it have been Papa Boutegourde?"

Miss Finney slammed down her empty glass and raised her hands in despair.

"God Almighty, Hoop," she said, "why couldn't it have been Santa Claus? But if you want a specific reason, César would never have made that mistake about the knife. He knows native customs backwards and forwards. He'd have done it right. Henri killed Gérôme."

I felt stunned and helpless. "There's a lot you haven't explained," I said.

"There's a lot I don't know," Miss Finney admitted. "I'm through talking for now, Hoop. I've got to rest. No—I can't. Take me back to Gérôme's, Hoop. I've got to write a letter."

I looked at her.

"That's right," she said. "A letter to Henri."

# CHAPTER SEVEN

## *How We Ended*

W HEN I WENT UP to the Boutegourdes' later that night to get a sandwich, Miss Collins was waiting for me with a message from Miss Finney. She said acidly that Mary had told her to tell me that she, Mary, had finished "that little job of writing" but wouldn't tell her, Emily, what it was. Maybe I knew; Mary seemed to tell me everything while certain other people weren't let in on it. And Mary wanted everybody, in the high-handed way she had, to be all packed and ready to leave from the Boutegourdes' for Costermansville in the morning. Mary said everybody *must* be there before seven, although we might have to wait until noon for her permission to leave. Nobody would be allowed to stay behind, but Mary had made no explanation as to why this was necessary. Miss Collins was breathless with resentment by the time she had delivered all this.

I said, "Your partner certainly takes over in a big way when she takes over."

Miss Collins turned on me like a field mouse protecting its litter and said, "Don't you *dare* say a word against Mary

Finney! She's a wonderful woman!" She pranced off in the direction of the kitchen to make my sandwich.

I hadn't intended to say a word against Mary Finney, but as I lay in bed that night I thought over all she had said about Henri, and although I couldn't deny that there was no place I could punch a hole in what she had worked out, I knew that Henri was a good man, and I wished that I knew the absolute straight of the thing, not just a synthesis of it as Miss Finney worked it up. I couldn't help knowing that however right she might prove to be in her facts, the very facts could lie about a man so that they distorted our image of him.

I went over to the Boutegourdes' according to orders the next morning. Miss Collins and Papa Boutegourde were all packed up and ready to go. Miss Finney came in half an hour later, looking grim, her mouth set in a hard line I had never seen on her face before. She drank a cup of coffee while the rest of us ate a decent breakfast to fortify ourselves, then she ordered Miss Collins and Papa Boutegourde into the station wagon, and said that when Jacqueline and Henri showed up, the four of us would follow in my truck and Henri's car. She said that if we didn't pass them on the road they should reserve rooms for everybody at the *Grand Hotel de Bruxelles* in Costermansville where Gaby and Madame Boutegourde were already supposed to be. One more thing, she said—if they saw a car coming up the road from Costermansville it would probably be the officials coming up to the station. They should try to wave this car down and tell the officials to look out for us, Miss Finney and me, on the road. She would tell them all about things, and come back to the station with them if necessary. This sounded phony to me, as did a lot of what she said with that new tight look of hers. But Miss Collins and Papa Boutegourde got into the station wagon without questions, and drove off.

Miss Finney said to me, "We'll give them an hour's start. I don't want to overtake them."

"Anyway we're waiting for Henri and Jacqueline," I reminded her.

"You know perfectly well we aren't," she said, but she spoke without her old snap. "We're leaving them behind." It was a grim ride to Costermansville. Miss Finney slept, or pretended to sleep, most of the way. Now and then we made desultory talk, avoiding any mention of anything we were thinking about.

We did meet the officials on their way up from Costermansville, four of them, their car parked at the roadside where Miss Collins and Papa Boutegourde had told them to stop and watch for us.

"No, you stay here, Hoop," Miss Finney told me, as I started to climb out of the truck after her. She made me drive ahead about forty feet and wait for her, but I could look back as I was parked there and I watched her talking to the men. Whatever she was telling them, she was getting a fine set of reactions. Her back was to me but I could see the faces of the men, amazed, incredulous, and full of concern. She talked to them twenty minutes or so, then I saw them lift their helmets to her with obvious respect, and she came back and climbed into the truck beside me and we went on. She remained quiet and unapproachable all the rest of the way to Costermansville except once when she reached into her pocket and pulled out a handkerchief and dropped it in my lap. I recognized it by the smear of blood that I had wiped off my hand that night. It had dried to its dull brown color. "Through with it?" I asked.

"I'm through with it," she said without expression. "I'm through with the whole thing." We rode on for a long time before she added, "I thought I might need that smear of blood if Henri destroyed his clothes, but I'm not going to after all." She wouldn't say anything more and when I threw the handkerchief out the window she made no comment. We got to the hotel in time for a late supper. When the others asked where Jacqueline and Henri were, Miss Finney told them they had gone back with the officials. After supper we went right up to our rooms.

Miss Finney stopped at her doorway and said, "Come in a minute, Hoopie."

I followed her in and she closed the door. She paced up and down uneasily for a moment or two and then went suddenly over to her suitcase and took out a fat white envelope. "You might as well have it now," she said abruptly.

Harshly, I would have thought, if I hadn't known she was covering up another emotion. "Let me give you the background. I wrote Henri that letter yesterday afternoon that I told you I was going to. I took it over to his house. Albert was still there. He said Henri was asleep, but wanted to be waked in an hour. I gave the letter to Albert and told him to give it to Henri when he woke him."

She paused, the white envelope in her hand, and I reached for it.

She drew it away. "Wait a minute," she said. "You know what I wrote in my letter. What we talked about yesterday afternoon. I also told him that if I found an answer to my letter in Gérôme's desk in the laboratory at seven o'clock this morning, we would all leave the station without him and Jacqueline. But that if I came there at seven o'clock and found him there himself instead of a letter, I would know there was something to talk over. Well, his letter was there. Here it is. I read it this morning before I saw you. You read it now."

She went over to the bed and lay down, turning her face away from me. I went over to a chair in the other corner of the room and took the letter out of the envelope. I still have it; Miss Finney let me keep it after they had photostated it for the records. It translates into this:

Dear Miss Finney:

You can imagine that I have difficulty in beginning this letter. I think it will be easier to continue with it. I want you to know the things you are curious about—not to satisfy your curiosity but in a way to justify myself. You have not asked for an explanation of what happened concerning Gérôme's death, but I can see that you are avid for it. Of course you are right in virtually all of your deductions concerning the death of

André. But I believe you have run away with yourself in exaggerating the callousness of my nature, and the extremity of the means I was willing to adopt when I found myself entangled in a desperate situation. Perhaps upon getting further away from the whole thing you would have begun to be less harsh in your assumptions. I am not trying to call myself good. I am not trying to appear altogether the victim of evil circumstance, or at all the tool of a vicious woman; I hope that anyone can see that I am man enough not to have been led wherever Jacqueline chose. But according to your present thinking it would appear to anyone that I had been. For that reason I am writing this to show you the truth, so that when this terrible business becomes known within the next few days, you will not spread any further your exaggerated idea of my villainy. I have not a great many friends in the Congo, and God knows what has happened to those I had in Belgium, but I would not want anybody to think any worse of me than I deserve, which is bad enough. I am even particularly concerned for the opinion of one person I know not well at all—the American, who must have received from all of us the most sordid and fantastic picture of life in our bush, that life which is usually sheer unromantic boredom, the marking of time until we can get back to civilization, but which at our station broke into such a nightmare of melodrama. The American is interested in native art; I have already given him my best piece, the ivory fetish, but if there is anything else in my house that he wants, will you see that he gets it? I cannot think of anybody else who would like to have anything of mine, unless Gabrielle would like the pictures on the living room wall that my brother painted, since Jeannette was fond of these. Everything of Jeannette's own I have destroyed, for the reason that you supposed. I wish that I had saved for Gaby the book of native legends she was helping Jeannette with. I know she would have liked having it, but I was destroying everything in a clean sweep. This is the last time I shall mention Jeannette in this letter, just as it is the last time I shall mention her in my life.

Your letter is mercilessly detailed and explicit. André discovered the relationship between Jacqueline and myself some months ago, no matter how, although you would enjoy hearing it. He was of course neither shocked nor resentful, having been what he was. I think that at first his strongest reaction was one of low-comedy amusement at his brother's cuckoldom. He had never liked Gérôme's living at his ease in Europe while André was sent to the Congo to rot away. I have always taken it for granted that André's family sent him out here as a young man because he was a wastrel at home. When the Company began to fail, André was pleased at his elder brother's misfortune in having to leave his good life in Europe for the hardships and monotony of the colony, but he was irritated when Gérôme began making serious efforts to reorganize the station, and to force André himself into some kind of effort and responsibility. Naturally André was delighted at the final humiliation of his brother—the discovery of Jacqueline's adultery—for I think André had also envied Gérôme the possession of a wife who so obviously excelled in the only quality which André demanded in a woman.

You are right that I was sick of Jacqueline, of her constant carping against Gérôme and the misfortune which had allied her to him, when actually she could have expected much worse from her life. I was sick of her jealousy, her frantic self-pity, and her hysterical demands as my mistress, which she regarded as a permanent alliance. I had never expected the thing to develop into more than the usual run of a hundred other affairs which begin the same way and end through sheer loss of momentum after the excitement of the preliminaries and the novelty of the first few weeks have passed. I think that if events had not taken the turn they did after André found us out, I would have chucked the whole thing and taken whatever consequences Jacqueline wanted to force.

André never asked me for money, but when he began to realize the weapon which had fallen to him, he began to amuse himself in a dozen ways. He began by coming to my house and carrying away whisky whenever he wanted it. He grew fond of making sluttish remarks for which I would ordinarily have hit him. He adopted the attitude that he and I shared a filthy secret, and when he could find Jacqueline alone his conversation was a stream of obscenities.

He came to my house one evening and asked for whisky and sat there drinking it. He revealed a depth of nastiness that I had never suspected, and hinted that I was expected to respond with technical descriptions of my intimacies with Jacqueline. I told him that he was not worth hitting like a man, and slapped his face. I told him that he could tell Gérôme what he chose and be damned. As far as its effect on myself was concerned, I had never cared whether André told Gérôme or not, since at the worst I would only have had to go through with an unpleasant scene and find a new job, which I was eager to do in any case. I would in fact have been cut loose from everything that bound me in this impossible situation, but I had some responsibility toward Jacqueline and I had nothing against Gérôme. I would have spared him this humiliation if André had not forced me beyond my limit.

Instead of going to Gérôme, André went to Jacqueline. She was frantic. Gérôme would divorce her without a penny; she had no dowry or property of her own, and she knew I had none to help her. André's asking price for his silence was what you have guessed it was, and Jacqueline agreed to meet him in Bafwali where Gérôme was sending him to pack up what was left in the house there. When she asked me for the dysentery culture I gave it to her, and if that is murder I am guilty of it. André did not seem human to me. Extermination is what I would call it.

When Jacqueline got back to the station last night she had seen you and knew that André had died, but she wanted to know exactly how things stood. Instead of going to Gérôme's she came to my house. That was when Gabrielle heard the car; it is difficult to judge the distance of sounds here at night, and she could not have heard the car anyway after it turned into the thick bush along my lane. Gabrielle must have been in her room, or on the bush path to the promontory, not to have heard Jacqueline leave in the car later.

It was true, as I told you, that I had gone to sleep early that night, but I had undressed and gone to bed. Jacqueline came to my room and woke me. She sat on my bed and I told her that everything had gone off all right. I saw no reason to tell her of your unusual interest in my dysentery cultures. She was limp with relief and said she was going to pour herself a drink. I told her she was taking a chance, that Gérôme might have been hoping she would arrive that night and could be listening for the car, but she was insistent. She brought back a drink for me too, and we were drinking them when Gérôme burst in on us.

My first feeling, and probably Jacqueline's, was that in addition to knowing now that Jacqueline had deceived him, Gérôme also knew she had poisoned André. That impression stayed with me through all the rush of events and confusion of that night, and in some illogical way it was terror of the peril in which this discovery would have placed us which helped sustain me through some of the things I had to force myself to do. It was not until later that I realized that André had no reason to suspect that he had contracted dysentery in anything but the usual way, so he could not have accused us to Gérôme.

Gérôme was white and trembling with shock and humiliation. I should have known that as fecal a nature as André's would have found one of its last pleasures in using the form of a death-bed confession to wound his brother with the pointless revelation of his wife's infidelity. Gérôme had not believed it at first, and then had tried to convince himself that André had spoken in some kind of delirium. He had made a point of referring to Jacqueline as casually as usual around the station, and he had asked me to dinner to see whether he could read anything from my attitude toward him as my host. He had spent days torn between his effort to rationalize back into their innocence a hundred circumstances which now appeared suspicious, and the mounting conviction that André had known what he was saying and had told the truth. And now he saw for himself.

Jacqueline lost her head completely and tried to answer that she had come to my house to discover whether Gérôme was all right before she went to him. Nothing could have been more ridiculous after two years of pretending that she wouldn't speak to me, and Gérôme gave it the wild laugh it deserved. He asked her if she couldn't see the whisky in her hand and her lover lying naked in his bed.

His trembling gave way to an access of fury and he grabbed Jacqueline by the wrists and dragged her from the room. By the time I had got up and pulled on a pair of pants I found them out on the veranda, close to the edge of the steps. He had her by the shoulders and was shaking her so that she snapped and twisted like a rag in the wind. I thought he was killing her, and I struck him hard enough so that he let her go and turned on me. Jacqueline slumped to the floor and when Gérôme lunged for me I hit him as hard as I could. I saw him fall backwards down the steps, then his whole body twisted over in a gyration that bent his neck under it, and he lay face down on the grass.

Jacqueline was sobbing for breath but I ran to Gérôme. I turned him over and felt for his pulse and his heartbeat. Jacqueline dragged herself gasping and choking down the steps and began beating Gérôme on the chest with both fists. I told her to stop, that he was dead.

So that was how it happened. We pulled ourselves together and got through the rest of that night on the reserves of strength that shock and terror unloose. I don't know how much chance I thought we had of successful deception, but there was nowhere else to try to throw suspicion except on the natives, and there was very little time to think things through. Jacqueline told me that she would make up her own story and plant her own evidence of Gérôme being attacked by natives; the less I knew about it the less likely I was to give it away inadvertently, she said. My whole story was to have been that I had slept through that night, simply that. I do not know yet exactly what Jacqueline told you about herself and Gérôme.

I got the body to the promontory and did to it what Gabrielle saw me doing, not with the circumcision knife, which was dull, but with my pocket jackknife, which I carried back with me and which served me on Dodo later. After that I threw it in the bush. The circumcision knife was Jacqueline's idea, and you are right, it was too much. If I had been anything but half crazed I would have known how inconsistent the knife was with what we wanted you to think the natives had done.

You know most of the rest. When I got back to my place I was too sick with horror and exhaustion to do more than sit down on the steps and cry with relief that it was all over. Dodo came out of her hut and stood at her stockade watching me. When I saw the lights of your truck down at the end of the lane I knew only one thing, that I had to explain the blood on my hands and my clothes. There was only one way to do it. Killing Dodo was as hard as anything I had to do that night. You stayed at the end of the lane for several minutes; it gave me time to get my rifle and fire it into the air twice. You were right about the eagle; he couldn't have waked me as I said, because he didn't scream until after you heard the shots.

I thought I was going to be able to hold out until you and Taliaferro had left me, but I got sick when you said I might have had worse than antelope blood on my hands. I have, so I am not sorry for what I have to do next.

Henri Debuc

When I felt able to speak, I said to Miss Finney, "Do you know anything more?"

She said, without turning her head toward me, "No, nothing more." Her voice gave out on her and it was a long time before she was able to say: "There's a lot of morphine in the laboratory. I hope they thought of doing it that way."

I have the things from Henri's house—the fetish he gave me, and the canoe paddles and the pottery and his other things. I have lent them, except for the fetish, to the University museum, where they are taking on that air of never having been alive that native work gets in a white man's museum. I hope someday to revive them when I have something more than a single room to live in. The circumcision knife went to the museum in Léopoldville after it was released from the files of evidence.

The Congo-Ruzi, moribund when I knew it, has ceased to exist. There were legal questions about the majority block of stock that came to Jacqueline from Gérôme. Jacqueline had no heirs. I believe there has been some kind of receivership appointed, but all that is left of the Congo-Ruzi as a company is some papers which are shuffled from lawyer to lawyer while their fees nibble away at the bit of remaining capital until before long it will have disappeared. As for the station grounds themselves, we thought for a while that the government might use them, but nothing came of it and I imagine that in the couple of years that have elapsed the bush has made a good start at taking over. I doubt that Henri's house is anything more by now than a few naked iron pipes.

I have had two letters from the Boutegourdes. The first was from Papa, written on a letterhead of the Colonial Agricultural Administration in Léopoldville, thanking me for my help in getting him a place as general supervisor of the wartime emergency agricultural programs. After my surveys I thought that the position should be created and Tommy Slattery recommended that it be set up, and he took my suggestion that Papa Boutegourde fill it. It has worked out well and should go on into a good peacetime job too. In his letter Papa Boutegourde was happy for Madame and Gabrielle, who were busy and flourishing in Léopoldville.

This must have been true about Madame and Gabrielle, because the next was not exactly a letter, but Gabrielle's wedding announcement. The Belgian name of her husband wasn't one that I recognized and I have never heard anything about him, but there was a Brussels address on the invitation along with the Léopoldville one, so I take it he was a good enough catch.

Miss Finney is a regular correspondent even if she is an unsatisfactory one. Every three months I get a letter from her, but they are all short, and always just about the same. The last one was rather mellower than usual, though. It came from the hotel in Costermansville and said:

> Hoopie dear—
> We have finished another of our rounds and are here at the Bruxelles again for a couple of weeks' rest. No changes. Emily will always be the same and so, I fear, shall I. I keep pumping the natives full of medicine and Emily keeps them up to scratch on their hymns. I have stopped arguing with Emily over the relationship of the body and the soul, because I'm sick of the first, and the second is my own business.
>
> We love you dearly,
> M.F.

Read on for the first chapters of the
next mystery in the series,
*The Cabinda Affair.*

# THE CABINDA AFFAIR

## CHAPTER ONE

THE FRENCH CONSULATE always gave the best parties in Léopoldville—mostly because all the parties in town had to be just alike except for the place they were given, and the French Consulate had the best place. At all the parties there would always be the same pastries, and very good ones, too, and the same whisky and soda. Mostly there would always be the same people and, since it was still hard to find clothes, they would usually be wearing the same things they had been wearing to all the other parties.

But the garden of the French Consulate runs out to the edge of the great bluff that drops off, straight down, into the Congo. The current is very fast there, because the river is already narrowing to go through the big rapids, where the waves splash up as high as a house. On a quiet night you can hear the sound from a considerable distance up the river. The coffee-colored water churns and swirls where the garden drops away. The garden is pretty, with thick green grass and a few rose bushes, and chairs and tables here and there, with Brazzaville a spectacular background on the opposite bank of the river, away over there, especially toward dusk when the lights begin to come on. The women are pretty against it, pretty and languid. They all do a lot of flirting of a bored, habitual kind, and you carry away the impression that they were dressed in trailing chiffon and big picture hats, although this is never so.

I had just got back that morning from a week's trip to Cabinda, and it had been quite a trip and I was tired—not the kind of tired that makes you want to go to bed, but the kind of tired that makes you want to go out and get rested by doing something different instead of lying in some room cooped up with your tiredness. In Léopoldville there isn't much you can do when you feel like doing something different, but the annual party at the French Consulate, on the *Quatorze Juillet*, was a kind of political-social obligation along with being the closest thing to high-life that the town had to offer. So I went.

The party was already under way, and everybody was already grouped into the same groups that formed themselves at all the other parties. It was exactly the same bunch that went everywhere, with a nucleus of all the consuls and their wives, of course, and every businessman who was making as much as ten thousand a year if he was French or Belgian, or, if he was Portuguese, twenty thousand. There was a very pleasant pigeon- cote murmur of voices, for there is nothing prettier to listen to in the way of human speech than the voices of women speaking French with the right kind of r's and u's when they are engaged in idle dalliance at a garden party.

I went down the line and made my little bow to the proper people, and as soon as I got away from the end of the line and started across the lawn to fall into one of the groups I always fell into, a boy handed me a drink, and while I was taking the first sip of it and looking out across the rim of the glass, I saw

Dr. Mary Finney standing off all by herself in one corner of the garden, with her big red freckled arms sticking out of a short-sleeved party dress and her big hands folded across her stomach, scowling uncomfortably at the rest of the party and looking like a carrot in the middle of an orchid corsage.

Miss Finney's carroty hair that went with the red freckles was hidden, but not under the old beat-up shoe-whitened sun helmet that was so much a part of her out in the bush where she really belonged. It was hidden today inside an indescribable object that on closer examination turned out to be a kind of white felt hat. She didn't have on the serviceable dun-colored dress I had always seen her in either; her party dress was a garment that had probably been designed to have some kind of lines to it, but it had never been designed to go with Miss Finney's lines or Miss Finney's dimensions. Not that she was a great big woman or a fat one, but she was definitely solid and hillocky, and the sleazy cloth with splashes of big bright flowers printed on it was stretched over her like a bad upholstering job, so that it bagged in some places and in others looked ready to burst its seams if she made an incautious move.

I had almost reached her before she saw me, but she didn't change expression when I came up, just went on glowering.

"Hello," I said.

She said, "Hello, Hoopie, for God's sake." I couldn't do anything but stand and grin. "What's so funny?" Miss Finney snapped.

"Nothing's funny. It's wonderful seeing you again, that's all. What are you doing in Léopoldville? They run you out of the Kivu?"

Miss Finney snorted, then said, "Can you get me out of here?"

"Maybe. Can you move in that dress, safely?"

The glare went away and she smiled. "I'm glad to see you too, Hoop," she said. "We got here three days ago and were awfully sorry to find you were away. Emily's around somewhere." Emily was Miss Emily Collins, another American. She and Miss Finney were itinerant missionaries, with Miss Collins working the soul-and-hymn department while Miss Finney ministered to the flesh. I don't know to this day whether Emily Collins was a D.D., but Miss Finney was an M.D. and a first-rate one.

"We're going home," Miss Finney said.

"Really home? All the way home?"

"Emily's home," she said. "Milford, Connecticut. It scares me to death. Connecticut, after thirty years of Africa."

"What's up? Have you been fired or something?"

"Certainly not! We're even going to get medals or something." She made a faintly wry face to show what she thought of medals or something.

"You're not going all the way back to the States just to collect a medal!" I said.

"No, we get the medals here," she said, "for service to the natives, if you can imagine that. But Emily's not well. And you know Emily. She thinks she has to go home and die. She's not going to die, but she thinks she is, so I'm taking her. I don't know, Hoopie—it seems very strange, after all these years." She sighed, drawing in her breath carefully. Some wrinkles in the dress filled up, then sagged again as she let the sigh out. "Damn it anyway," she said, "I'm so embarrassed I can hardly talk. Don't I look awful?"

I looked at her face and said, "On the contrary, you're looking unusually well, even for you."

"Don't try to fool me," she said. "You know what I mean. Sure, I'm well like a horse, as usual. I mean the dress. We've had to go to all these parties and things—we're even going to the Governor General's, to get the medals. So I went to the goddamn store, and I admit I'm a difficult subject but look what they did to me. I'd rather go naked." Her eyes wandered out over the garden, with all its pretty, dressed-up women.

"When you get that medal," I told her, "get it in that burlap creation and your sun helmet. The G.G. would love it. Do you really want to leave?"

"This party?" She gave another snort that should have withered all the surrounding foliage. Then she said to me, "But you just got here."

"I can see these people any time."

"You've got to say hello to Emily. She's somewhere."

"All right, we'll say hello to Emily, then there's something I want to tell you about. A long story. Something especially for you. All the time it was happening I kept wishing you were there. It was like that time at the Congo-Ruzi, when we—"

"Hoop!" She snapped to life for the first time.

"It just happened," I said. "During this past week. A real adventure. In Cabinda."

She cried, "Cabinda!" in a way that should have made me suspicious right then. "You mean to say you've been in—Come on, let's find Emily, then let's get out of here and ride."

We found Miss Collins off in another corner of the garden talking to a Father Simon, the head of the French mission school, and a couple of his teachers. Emily was sitting, primly as usual, on the edge of a concrete imitation of a marble bench from Versailles, with the particularly hesitant and apologetic air she always had when anyone paid any attention to her. She looked frailer than ever, and her little face was pale and grainy. I was surprised to discover how pleased I was to see her, because although I liked her fine I never really thought of Emily Collins as anything much more than a kind of appendage to Miss Finney, and this was an injustice because she had a lot of spunk to her underneath her timorous manner.

"Hoopie and I want to go now, Emily," Miss Finney said, after we had been polite all the way around to Father Simon and the others. "Have you got a car, Hoop?"

"I came in a taxi. We can get another."

Miss Finney interrupted and said purposefully, not looking at Emily, but straight at Father Simon, "Emily, do you think you can get back to the hotel if I take the wagon?"

"I'd be delighted to take Miss Collins to the hotel," Father Simon said.

"Really, Mary," Emily breathed. She coughed and pulled at the hem of her skirt. She hadn't changed a bit.

"Oh, thanks," said Miss Finney. "Well, goodbye, everybody." She gave a vague gesture that took in the whole group and strode off for me to follow.

Outside she had the same rickety old station wagon that she and Miss Collins had made their rounds in for years. "I couldn't bear to leave it behind," she said. "We put it on the lake steamer as far as Kisenyi and then drove it all the way to Stanleyville, then we put it on the river boat for the rest of the way."

"I'm glad you've got it," I said. "Seems like home." We had had some long talks in it.

We started riding, and I began telling her what had happened in Cabinda. First I did all the talking, but later on Mary Finney began asking questions and something remarkable began happening to my story. Under her scrutiny the events that I had thought were pretty obvious and logical began to stop making sense. Before I had finished, everything had fallen to pieces and I saw that things had been happening on one level while I had watched them from another. When I began talking to Miss Finney, I thought that the Cabinda adventure was an adventure already completed, that everything was wound up and tied off, but by the time she had examined everything that night, it turned out to be only half finished after all. We rode into the country as far as the good roads went in both directions, and circled all over Léopoldville again and again, and had dinner at a restaurant called the Petit Pont on the outskirts of town, then started over the same roads again, over and over. We stopped for a while on a parking place called Hippopotamus Point, overlooking the river, and then rode some more, with me talking all the time and telling the story that I am going to begin telling here. Everything that I told Miss Finney is here, a fact which I mention because Miss Finney was able to see in it, even in my telling, so much more than I knew was happening, because underneath the surface of what happened there was a lot going on that I didn't see. The only difference between the story as I am telling it here and the story as I told it to Mary Finney is that here I have to add enough in the way of explanation and comment to fill in the things about myself and about Africa that Mary Finney already knew and took for granted.

So this is the way the first part of it happened:

# CHAPTER TWO

AFTER BREAKFAST I WOULD always give myself
the treat of going back across the yard to my room and lying on
the bed to smoke a couple of cigarettes. In the yard the boys
would already be doing our wash and hanging it on bushes to
dry. If we didn't keep an eye on them, they would forget and
lay it out on the ground, but there's something or other you
can pick up that way—one of the thousands of little itching
parasites you pick up anywhere in the Congo, until you learn
the routine rules for keeping healthy. Whatever these little
itchy things are, they don't seem to get on the natives, or else
the natives don't notice them for all the other discomforts they
suffer, so our boys thought we were crazy to insist that our
clothes be dried on the bushes instead of being laid out on the
grass. I suppose they put it down to juju.

Breakfast was always a good meal. The morning would still be cool, and at that time of year there would always be papayas and avocados on the table. They were the sweetest papayas I ever tasted—too sweet for many people, but I liked them. The avocados were a little thready, compared with the creamy ones you get in California, but they were good, and I ate them with a lot of salt and pepper. The coffee was strong and bitter with the burnt chicory taste that I liked so much and that the other members of our mission always complained of. Papaya and avocado and black coffee were enough breakfast for me in that climate, unless there would be a piece of cold pie in the icebox left over from dinner the night before. If I had the pie, I would have an extra cigarette after breakfast, too. It was always pleasant to lie there smoking in what was left of the cool early hours. I would twist up the mosquito net, which hung from a hook in the ceiling so that it made a big tent at night, and push it back of a native spear that I had screwed onto the side of the headboard. I had a pleasant room—big and square and high-ceilinged, with a concrete floor that I finally learned to keep even grass mats off of, because of the bugs. I had all my masks and fetishes and so on arranged on improvised shelves all over one big wall. It made a pleasant room.

By the time I had finished the cigarettes, the comfortable part of the day would be over and, as soon as I got up, one of the boys would come in to make the bed.

But this morning I was still lying there when Felix showed up and told me that Tommy Slattery wanted me to come over to the office. Tommy Slattery was my boss, and Felix was our office boy. Altogether we had anywhere from a dozen to eighteen boys working for the four of us Americans all the time. We got good boys because we paid high—the cook got more than any of the rest of them, eight dollars a month. Theoretically we gave them their food too, but they didn't like European cooking even when they learned to do it well themselves but preferred to bring some evil-smelling lunches of their own, wrapped in banana leaves. The boys had a rigid caste system worked out among themselves—the cook wouldn't touch laundry, the laundryman wouldn't touch housework, the houseboys wouldn't touch yardwork, and so on, down to the half dozen little slaveys, the plantons, that the boys themselves sometimes hired for fifty cents a week and bullied into doing most of the work for them.

Felix was one of our best boys. His English was good enough to be usable, his French was good enough so that he could answer the phone, and he knew the local Congo dialects so that he could bargain for us when natives came around to the place from time to time selling fruit or eggs or curios. The Belgians complained that we spoiled our boys, and I guess they were right, because Felix ended up by stealing fifty dollars out of the office kitty.

I never saw him again after his arrest, but some of the house-boys testified against him at the trial and told us that he had been pretty well beat up in the jail. They gave this news with great relish because, next to the cook, Felix had been the highest paid of them all, and naturally they enjoyed seeing him get his come-uppance; the natives are jealous, cruel, and suspicious among themselves. Felix's wages were really enough to keep him in all he needed. He got fancy ideas, though, and had stolen the fifty dollars to buy a bicycle. He had also stolen a case of our whisky to get drunk on. You can get just as drunk on banana beer as you can on Scotch, which this was, but there was great prestige attached to getting drunk on regular white man's whisky, the white man's worst habits being the ones that were most admired and first imitated.

I put out my cigarette and went over to the office. We had a nice set-up—one house for the dining room and kitchen and guest rooms, and another one for our own bedrooms, this one a long boxcar-like series of rooms strung together so you had to go through the intervening ones before you got to the bathrooms at either end, and finally our offices, which took up a third converted residence. All these structures were entirely of concrete, impervious to ants and brand new, but so badly built that they were already settling and cracking, and designed in a sort of phony functional style that I called Contractor's Modern. The first half of Léopoldville was built in imitation of villas at Ostend, and the second half in this bastardized Corbusier stuff. It was a pleasant little city, though, with two daily newspapers, one functioning movie, and three ice-cream and pastry parlors. I grew fond of it.

We went over there during the war to buy things like tin and diamonds and so on, and after the war we were part of the WCSC, the War Contracts Settlement Commission, but what we were used for was just anything that came along, mostly. Tommy Slattery and I agreed on just about everything except what constituted an attractive woman, and I guess that is as sound a relationship as you can have with another man in the Congo, when you have to work with him and live with him and carry on a sort of Siamese-twin social life with him—to be in agreement with him on everything except which women you like best, since that is the most serious field of competition and limited supply, women. So we got on fine.

Tommy had his feet up on his desk and was finishing his own after-breakfast cigarette. He also had his after-breakfast highball on the desk beside him, and a bucket of cracked ice. I took a chair and Tommy said, "Morning, Hoop, what do you know about mahogany?"

"Since when are we interested in mahogany?" I asked.

"Since yesterday, it looks like," he said. "Could you recognize a kind of mahogany called Khaya? Is that the way you pronounce it?"

"That's right, Kah-yah. Yes, I could recognize it, but it's just a kind of generic name for mahogany, and—"

"I don't know what the hell generic means," said Tommy. He was a very direct person and always liked to do things the simplest way, and he never tried to bluff people he knew well or let anything go by that he didn't understand, step by step.

"Well," I said, "I mean there are lots of mahoganies all called Khaya, but if you asked me to distinguish one Khaya from another, I might get stuck on some of them."

Tommy picked up some pink sheets from his desk. They were our regular incoming cable forms that all our messages from Washington came to us on, through the Consulate, for decoding. Tommy looked over one of them and said, "This stuff is called Khaya Ivorensis."

"They can't get any Khaya Ivorensis around here," I said. "Ivorensis would be Ivory Coast Khaya. There's plenty of it in British West Africa and Nigeria. I imagine the British contract for all of it. If you're after Khaya Ivorensis we'd better get in touch with our bunch up there."

"This cable's from up there," Tommy said. "Not from our bunch, but from a new man, a man named Cotter. He's a lawyer and trouble-shooter in general assigned to Central Africa and he's going crazy. I think you're about to take a trip."

"What do you mean, he's going crazy? Really crazy?" It wouldn't have surprised me too much, because among the bright boys that the government agencies had sent all over South America and Africa and everywhere else in the world on missions like ours, I had seen some prize neurotics who hadn't been able to stand even the fairly mild gaff of strange food, rough climate, and the combination of working with Washington at too great a distance and the local boys at too close quarters. This isn't running down the personnel—they were really bright when I call them that, but when they were also theorists who had never done more than write books on economics, they got lost in a forest they couldn't see for the leaves. My own work was always easy, depending only on a good natural resistance to tropical heat, average common sense, and an ability to go slow.

"No," Tommy said. "Cotter's not crazy. He's one of the best men out here. Anyway that's what I hear. It's just another of those messes they expect us to straighten out overnight, and Cotter needs someone on our side who knows mahogany. They say he's a good guy—personally, I mean. He's also a hell of a bright lawyer. I don't know exactly what you're in for. Neither does Cotter, from these cables. The two of you will just have to work it out the best you can. Didn't you get any word on this mahogany stuff before you left Washington?"

"Not a word. Not on mahogany."

"Well, read these."

He gave me all the cables and sat quietly while I read them through. Then I said to him, "As far as I can tell, we're being asked to check on the fulfillment of a contract we've never seen. The only thing they're definite about is the date of delivery and the price. And the type of wood."

"What about the price?" Tommy asked.

"Unless prices have changed more than I think, it's outrageous," I said. "It's thirty percent higher than any price I've ever seen, and the log length is shorter than they usually allow. Somebody ought to make a pile of dough."

"Maybe," said Tommy, "except it sounds as if somebody's having trouble delivering." According to the cables, there had already been two long extensions on the date of delivery of the first load, and if delivery wasn't made by the 15th, which was only a week off, the contract would be cancellable.

"What about it from our point of view?" I asked Tommy. "Would we like to cancel it?"

Tommy gave a shrug of ignorance and said, "It was a war contract. The war's over. Ergo, or something like that, I'd say offhand that whatever we were going to use the Khaya for, we don't need it any more. But I don't know." He paused long enough for me to see that he was thinking twice before he said what he was about to say, then he went ahead and said it anyway. "I don't think the mahogany makes any difference one way or the other," he said. "I don't think it was primarily a mahogany contract."

"What, then? Some kind of swindle?"

"No, I don't mean a swindle," Tommy said definitely. "And I don't want you and Cotter to approach it as a couple of swindle-shooters or you'll run into trouble sure. But I don't think for a minute it's for Khaya, Ivorensis or any other kind. Not primarily."

"Then give. Expand. In words of one syllable."

"Good will," said Tommy. "I think it was one of those good will contracts. You know—good neighbors, buddy-buddy stuff, Uncle Sam, everybody's friend—dough, money, mazuma, coin of the realm. Love for sale. Did you notice this was in Portuguese territory?"

The only Portuguese territory I knew of in Africa was Portuguese Angola, below the mouth of the Congo but crowding up close to the little neck of Belgian territory where the river runs through to the ocean. The pink cables said the mahogany was in a place called Cabinda but I hadn't heard of it and I took it for granted that Cabinda was some little coast town in the mahogany-producing areas farther north. I said so.

Tommy allowed himself one smirk before he admitted that he hadn't heard of the place himself before the cables came in. I suppose you could crowd all the Americans who have ever heard of Cabinda into a decent-sized living room, if you left out trained geographers and maybe the State Department and a few missionaries. Tommy swung his chair around so he could point to Cabinda on the big map of Africa on the wall back of him. There it was, a little green spot, about the size of a piece of confetti on the big map, and only a hundred miles or so from us, a little tiny patch of territory on the other side of that narrow Congo corridor. It was the first time I had ever realized that both of those tight strangling borders were Portuguese.

"I think," said Tommy, "that some of our Belgian friends would have been very, very happy if Portugal had gone in with Germany. The Belgians might have tried to set up some territorial claim or other so they wouldn't have been stuck in here more or less like Floyd Collins. But you may remember that the United States was very, very anxious for Portugal to remain neutral."

"So was Portugal," I said.

"Okay," said Tommy. "Anyway, I think this contract must have been love for sale. Maybe we did need the mahogany, maybe not. You say it would be odd if there is really any mahogany growing there. Whether there's mahogany or not, the contract sounds like a funny one. You slug loads of dough into a funny little place nobody ever heard of for an obscure commodity and everything goes wrong with the terms of delivery and so on, and it sounds like everybody was just playing around with some kind of nominal arrangement when really it was love for sale. Is that clear?"

"I guess so. So now there doesn't seem to be much point in socking in all that dough. Is that your idea? If the contract does turn out to be cancellable, are those your instructions—cancel if possible?"

Tommy looked irritated, which he seldom did with me, and set down his highball glass and said very definitely, "No. My instructions to you are to look at the stuff and see if it's Khaya Ivorensis, deliverable under the terms of the contract as nearly as we can tell them from these lousy cables, and to do nothing more. Cotter's a lawyer and he's in charge and you're just a tropical products man who goes along to identify the wood. See? If anybody's nose has to get dirty, let it be Cotter's. And all this stuff I've been saying is only my own idea, not any kind of word from Washington or anywhere else. Is that clear?"

"It's clear from where I sit, but I'm not in Cabinda yet."

Tommy said, "You will be—you'll be there day after tomorrow. I called the Portuguese consul—got him out of bed. He's never heard of the contract but he's getting your visa ready, and a letter to a man named Falcão." He spelled it out for me. "With a funny thing over the second *a*," he added. "I can't find out anything about him except that he runs the *Companhia Khaya* in Cabinda—runs it as local manager, I mean, and he's a stockholder, but the really big boys are in Lisbon or somewhere. But it's Falcão you'll deal with. Your French visa is still good and you'll need it because you've got to go up through Pointe Noire first, and then drop back down to Cabinda. Don't ask me why. I suppose Cabinda just isn't the Monte Carlo of Africa and people haven't beat a very good path to it yet. I called the airport. You've got a ride as far as Pointe

Noire. That means tomorrow morning. After Pointe Noire you get there any way you can—you'll probably have to rent a car. Whatever you're doing here can wait. This shouldn't take more than a week, since that's the delivery deadline. I'll cable Cotter that you're meeting him at the biggest hotel in Pointe Noire, whichever hotel that is, as soon as he can get there. Have you got plenty of money?" I nodded. Tommy smiled. "That's everything, then," he said, "except those God-awful fetishes. Don't ring in more than a couple of extra days per diem while you do your collecting, and get as much stuff cleared off your desk today as you can."

"I'll get right at it," I said, but first I went back to my room and lay down again and had the extra cigarette that was still coming to me. I lay there thinking things over and I had the good relaxed feeling of anticipation that always came when I got a chance to get out of the office routines and go to a new place on a mission that involved several unknown factors. There were more unknowns than usual in this one, and one of them that was already coming to a head while I lay there smoking my cigarette was murder.

I finished my cigarette and then went out into the yard and told Antoine, who did my laundry, that I had to have all my khakis by that night, and all my white shirts too. I knew he would manage it somehow. I told him I was going in a plane and he asked me whether it was a male or a female plane. The boys were quite serious about this, having decided, I never have known why, that the DC-3s the ATC used were female, and the Lockheeds we got for Sabena, the Congo air line, were male. I told him a male plane, and he nodded his head and said that was good. If I had said female, he would have ducked his head and snickered. I never did figure this out, but that's the way it always was.

Since Tommy had asked me to clear my desk, I went in and wrote two or three letters that were more or less urgent, then made neat piles of everything else and put them in the desk drawers. Then I called our Consulate and they said my passport was ready with the Portuguese visa. I asked Tommy for the car, a sad old Dodge that we rented for a hundred and eighty dollars a month, and went down to the Consulate.

My friend Schmitty was sitting there at his desk in the outer office, with a big fat book open in front of him, looking resentful. Ordinarily Schmitty looked as if he were just passing the time between yawns, but this morning he looked resentful. He looked up at me as I came in and, being a very clean-spoken young man, all he said was, "You give me a pain in the ass." Schmitty was a tiny, wispy little fellow, an assistant-assistant consul or something of the kind, and made half my salary and never got any trips as part of his job.

"I like you, too," I said. "What do you know about Cabinda?"

"I'm an authority on it, as of today," he said. "It's something called an enclave. You can look that up for yourself if you want to. The enclave of Cabinda is governed from Angola through an officer called the *Intendente*. See? Well, this *Intendente's* named Machado and I don't know anything about him except that I've got to prepare a letter to him making the least of your short-comings."

"I see. What about the country?"

Schmitty leaned back in his chair and clasped his hands back of his head. He closed his eyes and recited, "Coastline of ninety-three miles; greatest breadth, seventy miles. That multiplies to 6,510 square miles, not even a good-sized ranch in Texas, but it's so narrow in parts that it has only half that area, less than half, about 3,000 square miles. It has towns named Cabinda and Landana and Massabi, and a river named the Chiloanga. That what you want?" He opened his eyes and caught me looking at the title of the big fat book. It was the *Encyclopaedia Britannica*, 13th Edition, Volume 15—Italy to Kyshtym.

"They spell it with a K here," he said. "You son of a bitch. It also says, quote, from the beauty of its situation and the fertility of the adjacent country, it has been called the paradise of the coast, unquote. That's the main town, Cabinda, they're talking about. Says it has a good harbor. I doubt that. It's old as towns go in these parts; used to be a hell of a slave port. And the write-up employs the word *whilst*."

"I want a copy of that write-up," I said.

"You're a fine big strong young man," he said, "and I'm undersized and underpaid. Copy it yourself. But it's lifted from a circular by the Cabinda Boosters' Association, if you ask me. I hope you die there, right on your per diem. How about some coffee?"

We went out and had coffee and pastry, and the next morning I left for Pointe Noire.

# CHAPTER THREE

POINTE NOIRE WAS A BIG, sprawled-out, fly-blown, ill-tempered town knocked flat on its back by the heat. I had seen it once before, during the war, in the period of French humiliation and discouragement. But even now, with the war over and the French victors, or nominal victors, Pointe Noire had the same half-sneering, half-indifferent air, and I decided that its *je-m'en-fouism* had become chronic. They say the French colonial is never happy, but I hope he's never more unhappy than he seems to be in Pointe Noire.

I put up at the Hotel Metropole in a room that smelled as if a family of cats had just moved out, and began waiting. There was no word from Cotter. At noon the hotel served a lunch of lamb stew that I was pretty certain was really nice ripe goat. Afterwards I tried my room again, but the heat had increased so that now it smelled as if the family that had moved out had been a family of vampire bats who had moved out in disgust, and it was so bad I had to go down to the lobby. The people sitting around dully at tables before glasses of tepid beer were depressing beyond endurance, so I left a note at the desk, which was also the bar, and sent out messages to a couple of other dens that had hotel labels on them, telling Cotter where I was in case we missed connections. Then I went out to rent a car to take us to Cabinda and found an old beat-up Chevrolet that looked like something rigged up out of sheet tin and discarded bailing wire, and I signed for it at the equivalent of eighteen dollars a day plus ten cents a mile with all gas, oil, and repairs at our expense. It was as good as you could do in those parts. I drove this maybasket out to the airport, which was hotter and dustier than the Metropole but less smelly, and waited there until around evening a plane came in and they lifted Cotter out of it.

So this was Cotter. He was green with air-sickness and yellow with atrabrine. The green was a sort of olive-green, because it had to show through a regular Southern California sun tan. You don't see much sun tan in Africa because every-body spends his time keeping shaded. Cotter was young, tall, rather thin and, even through the seasick look, exceptionally handsome in a slender, athletic, juvenile, curly-haired way. He wasn't at all what I had expected, and his movie-star good looks disconcerted me.

I took him back to town in the Chevrolet, which gasped and groaned and put out one long continuous death-rattle all the way. If you had to stop or slow down, you were enveloped by the fumes of half-burned gasoline and oil, and at these times Cotter would retch miserably. He also had stomach cramps and told me to hurry because he had bad diarrhea that he just hoped wasn't going to be a real dysentery. He was sick, all right.

When we finally got to the hotel, I told the woman at the desk to call a doctor and asked for adjoining rooms that didn't smell quite as bad as the one she had given me. To go upstairs you had to go out through a garden courtyard and up an exterior stairway. In the courtyard they were slaughtering some more goats, and the carcasses lay on the neglected flower beds, with the thick heavy blood dabbled all over the tangle of dried grasses and stunted marigolds that struggled there. The live goats were bleating and squealing, and Cotter's face contracted in a spasm of sickness. When we got to our rooms, he fell on his bed and lay there as if he never expected to get up off it again.

There was nothing I could do for him but keep quiet while we waited for the doctor. He lay there on his back with his eyes closed and the back of one hand thrown up over his forehead. I looked at him and wondered why I should be filled with unreasonable suspicion. It wasn't a face to be suspicious of, with its shortish, straight, well-shaped nose and full, firm mouth. The eyebrows and lashes were heavy and glistening brown, yet the beard was only a shadow across the chin, more like a boy's sprouting beard than a man's, leaving his cheeks smooth. His hair was a medium brown which was lighter now as if it were sunbleached, and cut just short enough to leave a little bit of curl, as if he had tried to get it short enough to do away with the curls entirely. But I couldn't help seeing that another quarter of an inch would have really done the job. He was vain of those curls and the rest of his good looks, and I already knew it.

I suppose I had expected Cotter to be more like Tommy, a good ordinary matter-of-fact-looking man, and here he was looking like a beach-club glamour boy with Bond Street luggage. My own canvas duffel bag and rucksack looked pretty rough, stacked in the corner of the room with his pale pigskin bags. But it was silly to feel suspicious of a man just because he carried expensive luggage in Africa and didn't look like what you expected, or just because he was fancy looking and you weren't. I called myself a damn fool and sat there waiting for the doctor. The green began draining out of Cotter's skin. He looked a lot better after half an hour, when the doctor finally arrived, but the hollows in the corners of his eyes were still the color of grapes.

The doctor had the same air of fretful indifference as the other Frenchmen in Pointe Noire. He stuck a thermometer into Cotter's mouth, took his pulse, asked him how often his bowels were moving, told him to eat lightly, as if you could eat any other way at the Hotel Metropole, and prescribed quinine and epsom salts, which he dug out of his bag and laid on the table. He collected an exorbitant fee and went out, leaving me to give Cotter his medicine.

I gave him the salts but he wouldn't take the quinine. It was all he could do not to gag on the salts, and he lay quietly for a few minutes on the bed until he was sure he wasn't going to lose them, then he told me he had pajamas in the larger of his bags and asked me to get them for him. In the bag I saw what looked like some fancy sport shirts, California style, and a white linen suit, immaculate, on a tricky hanger covered by a heavy oiled-silk envelope. I was glad we weren't sharing a room, since I was going to be a vulgar fellow sleeping in my drawers, if anything.

He got into his pajamas, revealing a thin, almost hairless body, like his smooth almost beardless face, that made him look younger than I thought he probably was—about thirty, around my own age. He crawled under the sheet and sighed with relief. "I'll be all right in the morning," he said. "I'd heard about French pilots—but my God!"

"You've got more than air-sickness to get over."

"If it's only the runs and not dysentery, these salts ought to fix me up. They have before." But he didn't look as if he was going to get fixed up overnight. "Don't worry," he said. "You won't have to play nursemaid any more."

"I'm not worrying about playing nursemaid," I said, "but I'm worrying about what happens if you get really sick. We'd be up the creek and no paddle for sure. I don't know anything about law, all I know is a little about woods. I hope I know enough."

"You could do this job alone," he said. "I'll show you all the stuff I've got from Washington. Such as it is. Later. It's a funny business. There's a lot going on they're not telling us about." He stopped talking and turned over on his side, and his knees drew up with the pain in his stomach. "I'm going to lose something," he said. "Help me down the hall."

I helped him down the hall and waited outside the door for him. When he reappeared he was able to get back to the room under his own power. He lay on the bed and grinned feebly, but he was feeling better, the way you do after you work up to it and get it over with for the time being.

"It still doesn't sound like my kind of job," I went on. "What makes you say I could do it alone?"

"The official part of it, I mean," he said. "The actual checking on delivery. It's only a kind of journeyman's assignment, in case they actually do deliver. If they don't deliver, that's where I come in. Probably end up in suits and countersuits and every other thing. But what we're going down for officially is to accept delivery of the first consignment of wood."

"Do you think they've got it this time?"

"If they haven't, they're really shot," he said. "They've had their last extension."

"Maybe you don't feel like talking any more now."

"It's all right. It's even a help."

"Then," I said, "why all this rush all of a sudden? Why do we get needled like this? They've had all these other long extensions and nobody worried very much. Now all of a sudden they deliver within the next five days or else. I guess I'm just asking what the hell it's all about."

Cotter looked at me a long time without answering, but I couldn't tell, from his smooth, polite gaze, whether he was wondering just how much to tell me, or whether he was organizing what he wanted to say. It was a real poker player's face, and it occurred to me how valuable his type of perennially juvenile good looks must be as surface cover for a thoroughly mature and shrewd operator. I had never met anyone quite like Cotter before. I had met plenty of people I knew I couldn't deal with because it was obvious from the first that I couldn't get within feinting distance of them, and I had met plenty I didn't trust, and I had met plenty I got along fine with, too, but I had never before met anyone who left me as completely uncertain of where I stood as Cotter did. The minute I began to feel suspicious of him I knew my suspicions were unreasonable, but the minute I felt the impulse to open up to him the way I would have to Tommy Slattery, something warned me to caution. One thing I was glad to remember, Tommy had told me to keep my own nose clean, even at the expense of Cotter's, if necessary, and I intended to.

I heard myself say suddenly, "The less I have to do with this the better I'll like it. If it's Ivorensis I can identify it, and that's all you brought me along for, isn't it?"

The words had come blurting out and I was aghast at the way they sounded, timorous and defensive. I was afraid Cotter was going to laugh, and I felt my face getting hot.

But he only said, "You could do the job without me, but I certainly couldn't do it without you. The wood has to be identified as the right kind, then the rest is so simple anybody could do it."

"Providing they make delivery, you mean."

"Yes, of course providing they make delivery."

"What constitutes delivery? What would I do then?"

He said, "Delivery just means you've seen the stuff. When they show you the felled trees, dragged up to the edge of a passable road or the banks of a navigable river, then we accept them and they're delivered, whether they ever get any farther or not. And there's not another mahogany contract in all Africa that gives terms like that. The whole thing's loaded with privilege."

"I'd like to see that contract," I said.

"So would I," said Cotter, pretty grim. "But they've cabled me most of the terms. If this man what's-his-name, Falcão, shows us the Khaya in the proper quantities and lengths, then they've made the first delivery and they get their first loan on the contract. They spend it on new roads and so on, opening up for the next delivery. Up to now they've been paying their own way. It's about the only normal thing in the whole contract."

"What's the loan?"

He gave an actor's pause for a moment, and then said deliberately, "One million dollars."

As soon as I could speak, I said, "There can't be that much Khaya in the whole area, deliverable or undeliverable."

"All the same," said Cotter, "that's only the first payment. It's a four-million-dollar contract."

I felt as if somebody had slugged me. "Are you trying to tell me that a four-million-dollar contract depends on us looking at a stack of wood and me saying Khaya Ivorensis?" I asked him.

"That's right," said Cotter.

I remembered Tommy Slattery and I said, "Then it's not really just a mahogany contract. What are we supposed to get for all that money?"

"It sounds like a lot, doesn't it? But look at it this way. Divide it by the population of the United States. It's only a few cents for each man, woman, and child."

"Okay, so it's only a few cents from each man, woman, and child," I said, "but I don't see why this Falcão guy or whoever it is he works for ought to get my little brother's ice cream cone."

Cotter laughed politely at this, but he was getting tired again. "I suppose Falcão will come in for a lot of ice cream cones out of the deal," he said, "but a lot of the four million will go into roads and harbor improvements and so on. The harbor's full of Congo silt right now. It's a mud wallow."

"Then," I said, "Portugal dearly loves us because we develop Cabinda for them."

"In a way," Cotter said. "Something like that, perhaps." He leaned back and closed his eyes, and I should have stopped talking right away. But I didn't.

"Four million dollars," I said. "That's a lot of good will."

"Not really," Cotter murmured, sounding tired and weak. "It's very small potatoes, really."

"Four million dollars is? Small potatoes? Even for such a small place?"

"Very small," Cotter said, "compared with what goes on everyplace else."

"Four million dollars," I said again. "I wonder if anybody would be interested in my good will for, say, about a dollar ninety-eight?"

Cotter opened his eyes to look at me and said, "I wouldn't be surprised if you got a much better offer than that within the next few days."

"I'm not in the market."

"I didn't mean I thought you were. But you're in Africa, and I think Falcão is going to have trouble delivering. Khaya is a little word, short and easy to say. As you point out, all you have to do is say it and they get their money." He stopped, then in a minute he said, "If they're caught short, they'll be desperate. They'd give a lot, do anything—" but he was so tired now that he stopped again, and I saw he wanted me to go away.

"You'd better rest," I said. "I'll stick my head in now and then to see if you're all right. Maybe you can eat something after a while."

Cotter said, "You're very kind. I'm sorry to be such a weak sister."

He closed his eyes again and I left him there.